"There *is* one more thing."

"You're pushing your luck, Serena."

Pete looked tough, forbidding, and Serena wondered afresh whether she was insane to think she could handle this man. He walked his own path, made his own rules. But this last rule was important. "We need to be discreet."

He laughed at that, and the rich, dark sound of it slid along her skin like water.

"You're right," he murmured. "We'll be discreet." And then his lips were on hers, hard and seeking, and all her carefully thought-out rules shattered beneath the weight of her desire.

Pete's body betrayed him the moment he reached for her. He'd known it would. He could be discreet. If that was what she wanted. He'd do it.

Just as soon as he'd finished feasting on her mouth.

kept for his
Pleasure

She's his mistress on demand!

Whether seduction takes place in his king-size bed, a five-star hotel, his office or beachside penthouse, these fabulously wealthy, charismatic and sexy men know how to keep a woman coming back for more! Commitment might not be high on his agenda—or even on it at all!

She's his mistress on demand—but when he wants her body *and* soul he will be demanding a whole lot more! Dare we say it…even marriage!

Don't miss any books in this exciting miniseries from Harlequin Presents®!

Kelly Hunter

THE MAVERICK'S GREEK ISLAND MISTRESS

kept for his
Pleasure

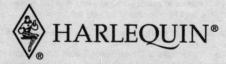

HARLEQUIN®

TORONTO • NEW YORK • LONDON
AMSTERDAM • PARIS • SYDNEY • HAMBURG
STOCKHOLM • ATHENS • TOKYO • MILAN • MADRID
PRAGUE • WARSAW • BUDAPEST • AUCKLAND

Recycling programs
for this product may
not exist in your area.

ISBN-13: 978-0-373-12825-9
ISBN-10:   0-373-12825-8

THE MAVERICK'S GREEK ISLAND MISTRESS

First North American Publication 2009.

Copyright © 2008 by Kelly Hunter.

www.eHarlequin.com

Printed in U.S.A.

All about the author...
Kelly Hunter

Accidentally educated in the sciences,
KELLY HUNTER has always had a weakness
for fairy tales, fantasy worlds and losing herself
in a good book. Husband...yes. Children...two
boys. Cooking and cleaning...sigh. Sports...
no, not really, in spite of the best efforts of her
family. Gardening...yes—roses, of course.

Kelly was born in Australia and has traveled
extensively. Although she enjoys living and
working in different parts of the world, she still
calls Australia home.

Visit Kelly online at www.kellyhunter.net.

CHAPTER ONE

THERE was a lot to be said for spending a day sitting beneath a striped blue and white beach umbrella on a little Greek island. Serena Comino, however, had been sitting beneath this particular beach umbrella every day for five months now—renting fifty cc motorbikes to tourists—and there wasn't a lot to be said about it any more.

The view never changed, as glorious as it was. The faces of the tourists changed with each docking ferry but their desires stayed the same. Get wet, lie on a beach, rent a Vespa, eat… Nothing *ever* changed.

Five months. Only one more month to go until she returned to Australia and the Greek-Australian arm of the family, or better yet *didn't* return home to the family bosom at all. Serena leaned back in the rickety director's chair until the front two legs left the ground, her eyes shaded by sunglasses, her head tilted towards the vivid blue sky beyond the umbrella. Maybe it had grown somewhat more interesting in the last five minutes. A passing cloud, a bird, a plane.

Superman.

Nope.

'Who suggested this?' she muttered.

'Your father,' said an amused voice from the direction of the goat track behind her. The track started at the edge of the village and meandered up the hillside, past her grandparents' rambling whitewashed cottage, and on to the road above, where Serena and the Vespas spent the better part of the day.

'Sad, but true.' She turned her head, a minimal movement, and offered up a smile for Nico, her cousin on her father's side, which meant the Greek side. The details weren't important, they were related. And it was their turn to pull carer duty for their eighty-two-year-old grandparents, not that they needed nursing care, for they were in remarkably good health. No, truth was, she and Nico were here to run the business enterprises Pappou refused to surrender. Nico's working day started at four a.m. on the fishing trawler and finished around lunchtime. Serena's started at nine, finished at five or six, and didn't involve fish. She still thought she had the better deal. 'Lunchtime already?'

'If you wore a watch you'd know.'

'I can't wear a watch any more,' she countered. 'Once upon a time when I had places to go and things to do I wore a watch. Now it's just too depressing. What's for lunch?'

'Greek salad, calamari, and Gigia's pistachio baklava.'

Okay, so there were some advantages to small Greek islands after all. She sat up, the front two legs of her chair hitting the dirt with a thud, and looked around to see why Nico hadn't taken his usual seat in the chair beside her.

He wasn't alone. A tall black-haired man stood

beside him with the body of a god and a smile guaranteed to make any woman look twice. Serena only looked once but made up for it by taking her time. Not Superman, she decided finally. Superman was square of jaw and neat as a pin. Wholesome.

This man was what happened when Superman took a walk on the wild side.

'Do you fly?' she asked him.

'Yes.'

'I knew it. Women can sense these things.'

'What's she talking about?' he said to Nico. He had a great voice. Deep. Dreamy. Amused. Australian.

'Does it matter?' she countered. 'Are we caring about that?' She sent him a smile she knew damn well could make a man tremble. He countered by removing his aviator sunglasses to reveal eyes as bright and blue as the sky above. Impressive. She stared at him over the top of her sunglasses to see if the tint was making them brighter than they actually were.

Nope.

'Rena, this is Pete Bennett. Pete, my cousin Serena. Her heart is pure. Much to the family's dismay, the rest of her is pure sin.'

'Serena.' Pete Bennett's smile was lazy, very lazy, his eyes appreciative without being bold. Superman-for-bad-girls knew women. Knew how to woo them, knew exactly how to play them. Always a bonus. 'That's quite a combination.'

Serena felt her smile widen. 'So I'm told.'

Sighing, Nico shoved the lunchbox in her line of sight and when that didn't draw her attention away from the delectable Pete Bennett he stood in front of her and blocked the view completely.

'Thank you,' she said begrudgingly as she reached for the lunchbox.

'You're welcome,' countered Nico dryly, everything about him telegraphing a warning about flirting with handsome strangers, even ones he'd just introduced.

Nico was all Greek and wholly protective of the womenfolk in the family. Serena was half Australian and born and raised in Melbourne, and his protective streak rankled even as it amused her. 'So…' Given that the flying one wasn't here for her entertainment he was probably here for business. She put the lunchbox beside the chair, got to her feet, and set about taking care of it. 'Care to rent a Vespa, Pete Bennett?' He looked like a man who appreciated a lick of speed. Not that a fifty cc two stroke was going to provide a great deal of that. 'It just so happens I can let you have the second fastest bike on the island.'

'What happened to the fastest bike?'

'That would be my ride.'

'He's not here for a bike,' said Nico.

'Then why *is* he here?'

Pete Bennett answered the question himself. 'I'm looking for a room.'

'Tomas's room,' added Nico.

Tomas was the grizzled old charter helicopter pilot who had first claim on the bedsit at the back of her grandparents' cottage whenever his customers elected to overnight on the island. 'Tomas's helicopter landed first thing this morning and hasn't left yet,' she countered. She knew this on account of her close personal relationship with the sky. 'What happens if *he* wants to stay over?'

'Tomas is in hospital with his leg broken in two places,' said Pete. 'I'm filling in for him for a time.'

'Oh.' Serena felt a slow smile begin to spread across her face again, she couldn't help it. 'You really can fly. As in forty-five minutes to Athens. Five hours to Rome. I'm *very* impressed. Why didn't you say so earlier?'

'I did,' he said, and to Nico, 'How long has she been here?'

'Too long.' Nico eyed her narrowly. 'And she doesn't always stay in the shade.'

Pete Bennett's lips twitched and Serena favoured both men with a narrow eyed glare of her own. 'The *shade* is the size of a postage stamp. This *island* is the size of an envelope. *You* sit here for five months solid and see how well you cope.'

'I offered to swap,' said Nico. 'I offered to mix it up. A day on the boat here and there, but no…' He shook his head sadly. 'The daughter of a Melbourne fishmonger with family holdings that include three trawlers, six seafood outlets, and two restaurants, and she doesn't like fish.'

'You don't eat fish?' asked Pete Bennett.

'Wash your mouth out,' she said. 'I just don't like catching and preparing fish, that's all. Gutting them, scaling them, boning them, that sort of thing. Nothing wrong with *eating* them. We do a lot of that around here.' But back to business. 'So you want the same deal as Tomas?'

'That's the plan,' he said. 'If it's all right by you, that is. Nico wanted to run it past you before he agreed.'

'Fine by me.' Serena slid her cousin a sideways glance. 'You didn't need to ask.'

'He's younger than Tomas,' said Nico with a shrug. True.

'And single,' said Nico.

Serena felt her lips tilt. The good news just kept coming.

'Might set tongues wagging, what with the grandparents away and me leaving for work so early in the mornings,' said Nico next.

There was that. But she was feeling rebellious when it came to the gossip mafia. She'd done *nothing* but behave since coming to the island and still the gossips watched her every move as if she were about to run amok at any minute. 'Let them wag.' She eyed Pete Bennett speculatively. 'Although we may need to tweak the deal somewhat to preserve my honour and accommodate your youth. I usually make Tomas's bed up for him. You can make your own.'

'Oh, that's cruel.' Pete Bennett shook his head and turned to Nico. 'I thought you said she had a good heart?'

'I lied,' muttered Nico. 'Take it as a warning. Women are cruel, as cruel as the sea and twice as unforgiving. Sirens all of them, luring innocent men to their doom.'

Definitely *not* Nico's usual take on the world. Usually Nico embraced the notion that women were there to be cared for. He had a sweet streak a mile wide, did Nico. Thoughtfully, Serena studied her cousin. He looked much the same as usual. Same kind brown eyes, strong handsome face, and sinewy body. The unhappiness lurking within those eyes, however, ran deeper than usual. 'You've been arguing with Chloe again,' she deduced finally. Chloe ran the island's largest hotel and was the bane of Nico's otherwise peaceful island existence.

'Did you hear me argue?' Nico asked Pete. 'Did I make any comment whatsoever that could be construed as an argument?'

'Nope,' said Pete with a shake of his head. 'You did not.'

'Uh-huh,' she said. 'So what exactly *weren't* you arguing about?'

Nico scowled. 'The usual.'

Which meant they'd been arguing about Chloe's nephew, Sam. No quick fixes there. 'How bad was it?'

Nico looked away, looked out to sea. 'Breeze is picking up. Figure I'll take the catamaran out this afternoon. Don't wait dinner for me.'

Bad. 'I'll save you some,' she told him. 'And make sure you eat it when you come in.'

Nico looked back at her and this time his smile did reach his eyes. 'Tomorrow I'll bring you another beach umbrella. A bigger one.'

He would too. 'And dinner with pilot Pete here? Shall I feed him or send him down to the village?' Tomas usually ate with them. Pilot Pete might have other ideas.

'I trust him.' Nico shot a warning glance in Pete's direction. 'A man of honour would not abuse my hospitality.'

'Are you a man of honour, Pete Bennett?' she asked him.

'I can be,' he said with another one of those lazy grins that made breathing a challenge.

'I'll dress platonic,' she told him. Honourable or not, she was looking forward to his company at dinner.

'Appreciated,' he murmured.

'Dinner's at seven,' she said as a pair of likely customers rounded the bend of the road and headed towards them. 'The kitchen door's the one on the other side of the courtyard, directly opposite your door. The picnic table in the middle of the courtyard's the dining room.' She slid him a parting smile and started towards the tourists, trying to gauge where they were from. Their top-of-the-line Mercedes-quality sandals and backpacks were a dead giveaway. 'I'm thinking German,' she muttered.

'Dutch,' countered Superman, *sotto voce*.

They'd soon find out. *'Yassou, Guten mittag, Goede middag,'* she said cheerfully.

'Goede middag,' they responded with wide white smiles, Dutch all the way to the tips of their German-made sandals.

Bugger.

Pete Bennett settled into the granny flat out back of the little white cottage on the hill with the ease of someone with wanderlust in his soul and no fixed address.

He'd been born and raised in Australia and he still called it home, no question. It was home to childhood memories, good and bad. Home to working memories too, some of them uplifting and some of them downright tragic. Not that it was the memories that had driven him away from Australian shores. No, he wouldn't say that.

He preferred to call it exploring his options.

Pete showered away the dirt of the day beneath a

lukewarm drizzle from an ancient showerhead and dressed casual in loose khaki trousers and a white T-shirt. If the goddess could dress platonic then so could he. Besides, it was the only change of clothes he had. He checked his watch, not quite seven, grabbed his damp towel from the bed, and stepped outside, heading for the single strand of washing line strung between two poles.

Movement at the edge of the grassy garden area warned him that he wasn't alone. A small boy with black hair, big eyes, and a narrow, pinched face stood at the edge of the garden. The same boy Nico had taken under his wing down at the fishing dock earlier that day until the fiery-eyed Chloe had come for him. 'Nico's not here,' he told the boy.

'Doesn't matter,' said the boy with a shrug, finding a home for his hands in the pockets of his ratty board shorts. 'Looking for you.'

Pete slung his towel over the line and reached for a peg, wondering just why the kid would be looking for *him*. The boy would get around to revealing what he wanted sooner or later. That or head back to wherever he'd come from. 'You've found me.'

'You saw what happened earlier,' said the kid after an awkward pause. 'I thought maybe you could talk to my *aunt*.' The last word was dragged from his mouth as if he resented the family connection with every fibre of his being. 'You know…' added the kid when he stayed silent. '*Chloe*. It's not as if wanting to work on a fishing boat is a bad thing. She oughta be *glad* I want to pay my own way.'

'How old are you, kid?'

The boy scowled. 'Eleven.'

Small for eleven. But the eyes were older. Pete thought of the luscious Chloe, who'd torn strips off Nico's hide earlier that afternoon when she'd caught the boy helping him unload the day's catch. Thought of the way Nico had listened in stoic silence, his silence giving the boy hope and his eyes promising *Aunt Chloe* retribution in the not too distant future. 'Why would your aunt take any notice of me?' Why for that matter was *she* riding herd on him instead of his parents? 'I'm a stranger here.'

The kid shrugged. 'She might.'

'Why not ask Nico to talk to her? He knows you. Hell, he knows you *and* your aunt.' And all the politics involved. 'I'm assuming it's Nico's boat you want to work on?'

The kid nodded. 'She won't listen to Nico. All she does is fight with him.'

He'd noticed.

'But you...you got no percentage either way.'

'Exactly.'

'She'd listen to you without getting angry about other stuff.'

Pete ran a hand around the back of his neck and looked to the sky for inspiration. The boy reminded him of his younger brother just after their mother's death. He had that same mix of defiance and vulnerability about him and it got to him, caught at him, and tugged at memories best forgotten. 'The way I figure it, you still have a few years of schooling left before you can leave. The way I figure it, going to school is non-negotiable.'

The boy's scowl deepened.

'Doesn't mean you can't try and strike some sort of deal with your aunt when it comes to your free time though. A kid like you knows how to deal, right?'

'Maybe.'

'So you tell her you'll go to school next week—no nicking off at lunchtime to meet the boats—if she'll let you work for Nico next weekend. *If* he'll have you. You tell your aunt you haven't talked to Nico about it yet, got it? Maybe you'll save him some grief.'

'Got it,' said the boy.

'On the other hand, Nico can probably fend for himself so don't sweat it if she does skip straight to thinking this was his idea. He might enjoy telling her it wasn't.' There, he'd done as much as he could for both Nico and the boy. Got way more involved than he ever intended to.

'Yeah, well…' The boy looked away. 'Thanks.'

'No problem.'

Pete watched as the boy lit off down the hillside towards the village, half sliding, half striding down the rocky track. 'Hey, kid…' The boy skidded to a halt and looked back at him wary and waiting and so damn vulnerable it made his heart ache. 'I'll be around some, these next few weeks. Let me know how it goes.'

The boy nodded, once, then he was gone.

Pete was three strides away from the bedsit door before he felt Serena's eyes on him. Two before he spotted her standing just inside the kitchen doorway, half hidden by the fly-screen door. 'You can come out now,' he said, cocking his head in her direction. 'You could have joined us before, come to think of it.'

'What? And interrupt all your good work? I don't think so.' She emerged smiling and unrepentant, a vision of sensuality from the tips of her bare feet, up and over her white gypsy skirt and sleeveless pink stretch top that revealed more creamy skin than it covered, to the glorious tumble of chocolate-coloured curls that fell to her waist. Pete Bennett knew women, lots of women. Beautiful, funny, intelligent women, but not one of them could even come close to the one standing in front of him for undiluted sex appeal and staggering impact on a man's senses. She sauntered—clearly there was no other word for it— over to a small silver coloured garden tap and started filling the bucket beneath it before sliding him a sideways glance from beneath long, dark lashes. 'His name's Sam.'

Pete filed the name away for future reference and regarded the goddess of buckets and sensuality curiously. 'Where's his father?'

'The wording on his birth certificate says "Father: unknown".'

'His mother?'

'She died in an Athens boarding house nearly a year ago of hep C. As far as anyone can gather, the only person looking after her was Sam.'

Rough. Damn rough on a kid. 'Is the Chloe who came down to the harbour to find him this afternoon his real aunt?'

'Yeah.'

'So where was *she* when her sister got sick?'

'You sound a touch judgemental.'

'Feels about right,' he said mildly. Given the picture she was painting.

'I *do* like a man who's in touch with his feelings.'

'Let's not get carried away,' he said dryly.

Serena turned off the tap, picked up the bucket and strolled towards a cluster of herbs by the kitchen door. 'Chloe was right here, running the hotel. She hadn't heard from her sister in over a year and a half.'

'Close family.'

'You're being judgemental again,' she told him.

'Uh-huh.'

'I like that about you.' A tiny smile played at the edge of her lips. 'Where was I?'

'Aunt Chloe.'

'Oh, yeah. According to Chloe, her sister lit out for Athens some twelve years ago, defiant, disowned, and three months pregnant. She was sixteen. Chloe was thirteen at the time and tried to play peacemaker. She failed. Her parents were unmoveable and her sister didn't want either Chloe's pity or the savings she sent her. The family fractured.'

'How'd the boy end up here?'

'Chloe's sister named her next of kin.' Serena shrugged. 'Chloe loves Sam, but she can't handle him. Sam's carrying a lifetime of rejection and an ocean of resentment around on his shoulders. He's fiercely independent. Chloe's fiercely overprotective. She's determined not to fail him. They clash.'

'So where does Nico fit into all of this?'

Serena chuckled, her expression lightening as she gave each clump of herbs a drink. 'Smack bang in the middle; between a boy who desperately needs to feel worthy and a woman he's crazy in love with.'

Pete shuddered. 'No wonder he's gone sailing.'

'You underestimate my cousin, flyboy. My money's on Nico claiming them both before summer's out.'

'It's a pretty picture to be sure.' So was she. 'Tell me,' he drawled. 'What would you have been wearing if this *hadn't* been a purely platonic evening meal?'

'Lipstick for starters.'

She didn't need it.

'And probably a dress.'

'Strappy?'

Definitely.

'Short?'

'No. Something demure. Just above the knees. A first-date dress.'

'What colour?'

'For you? Blue. So that when you looked at me you'd think of something you already loved. The sky.'

'Oh, you're good,' he said in admiration.

'Yes, I am.' Her accompanying grin rammed that particular point home. 'Now you. If this wasn't a strictly platonic dinner deal where would you have taken me?'

'For you?' He didn't have to think hard. 'The Trevi Fountain in Rome. I'd buy you a gelato and give you a bright new penny so you could toss it into the fountain and make a wish. And then we'd walk wherever our feet took us—a sidewalk trattoria or a bustling restaurant—and everyone in the room, myself included, would say a heartfelt prayer of thanks for beautiful sirens in sky-blue dresses.'

'Oh, you're *very* good,' she said wistfully.

'Thank you. I aim to please.'

'I'm sure you do,' she murmured as she slid the bucket back beneath the tap. 'You interest me, flyboy, I'll give you that. There's just one thing I can't quite figure out. Something that doesn't quite fit your carefree and extremely appealing image.' She smiled archly and sent a shaft of heat straight through him. 'What you said to Sam…the way you listened to him, helped him…the way you told him to get back to you.' She turned and headed for the door with a sway to her hips that was truly distracting. 'It was nice.'

CHAPTER TWO

NICE? *Nice?* Pete Bennett had been called a lot of things by the women who sauntered through his life, but *nice* had never been one of them. It didn't feel like a compliment. Okay, so he could, on occasion, be nice. Nothing wrong with that. But what if *nice* mutated into *caring*? What if caring morphed into *really* caring? Then where would he be?

Nope. Better to disabuse the bucket goddess of all nicehood fantasies immediately. Rolling his shoulders back for good measure, and with the spell she'd woven about him still clouding his mind somewhat, he headed across the courtyard after her.

The kitchen in the whitewashed cottage consisted of a fridge, a sink, a wall full of shelving laden with fresh food and a square central bench that doubled as a table. Simple, cosy, and, to Serena's way of thinking, all about the food. She'd put a chicken—liberally seasoned with garlic and oregano—in the oven earlier, along with half a dozen salt-licked potatoes. A loaf of crusty bread and the fixings of a salad sat on the bench waiting to be sliced, diced, and tossed into a bowl just before serving. Serena came from a family of cooks, chefs, restaurateurs, and foodies. Cooking might not have been her first love, or even her second, but in her family there was *no* excuse for poor cooking.

Pete had followed her into the kitchen and now stood leaning against the doorframe. Judging by the dangerous gleam in his eyes, he'd used up his daily quota of *nice* on Sam. Serena didn't mind a bit.

Nice was a bonus, certainly, but sexy, playful, and thoroughly entertaining would do just fine.

'Call me curious,' he said, 'but if renting Vespas to tourists isn't your lifelong ambition, why do it?'

'Family,' she muttered, taking a chunk of feta from the fridge and setting it on the bench alongside a wickedly sharp cutting knife. 'All the grandchildren do a six-month stint helping out here. It's my turn.'

'What happens when all the grandchildren have had a turn? Does it rotate back to the beginning?'

'Theoretically, that's when the great-grandchildren step up. Unfortunately, the oldest great-grandchild is currently six and Nico and I are the last of the grandchildren. I think everyone was hoping one of us would fall in love with the lifestyle and offer to stay on indefinitely. Nico might,' she said thoughtfully.

'But not you?'

'No. One more month and I'm gone.'

'Where?'

"Well, now, that will depend on the jobs going at the time.' And her chances of landing one of them. 'I'm a photographer by trade. When it comes to education I majored in languages, with a slice of international politics on the side.'

He didn't look as astonished as some. The ones who thought that, with a face like hers, she was far more likely to be on the other side of the camera. The ones who thought that, with a body like hers, brains were an unnecessary extra. 'Right now I'm working on a postcard series for the Greek tourism authority but as soon as I finish my stint here I'll be chasing a photojournalism slot, preferably with one of the global media groups.'

'You'll do well,' he said.

'I will?' She couldn't quite hide her astonishment. Not the usual reaction when she told someone her plans.

'Yeah. Your looks will get you noticed, your intellect will tell you when there's a story to chase, and your people skills will get you the information you need. It's a good choice for someone with your particular skill set.'

Serena sliced the bread, sliced the cheese and stuck them together before holding it out to him with a smile. 'Just for that you get an appetiser. Possibly even dessert.'

He took the sandwich with a grin. 'I hear it's a very competitive field. You'll need ambition as well. How bad do you want it, Serena?'

Bad enough to have queried every major global newspaper and some not so global ones about upcoming positions every month for the last five months. 'Trust me, I've got the ambition thing covered. Maybe in the past I've let family commitments keep me from pursuing this type of career, but not this time. This time I'm determined to get where I'm going.'

'Just as soon as you get off this island,' he said with a hint of dryness that she chose to ignore.

'Exactly.'

'So technically speaking, apart from the Vespas, the postcard photography, and keeping an eye on your grandparents, you're a free agent this coming month.'

'That's me.' Damn but he was appealing. 'And my grandparents are visiting both sides of the family on the mainland at the moment. They left this morning, so you can count them out of the equation for a couple of months. You?'

'I'll be flying these skies until Tomas recovers the use of his leg. Six…eight weeks. Maybe longer.'

'And then?'

He shrugged. 'There's an offer from an Australian mining company to run a charter-flight operation for them in Papua New Guinea. It's a good offer.'

'Yes, but is it ethical?'

'What they're doing or what I'd be doing?' he countered with a quick smile, and Serena figured she had her answer.

'So you flit,' she said dryly. 'From one flying job to another.'

'I like to think there's a big-picture plan somewhere in amongst it all,' he said mildly.

'Ever thought about settling down?'

'You mean some place permanently or with a woman?'

'Either.'

'No.'

Serena closed her eyes, muttered a prayer. As far as potential short-term romantic interludes were concerned, the man was utterly, mouth-wateringly perfect.

'Did you just whimper?' he said, eyeing her closely. 'I thought I heard someone whimper.'

'No whimpering here.' Much. 'What can I get you to drink? Water, wine?' She gestured towards the glass of white wine already on the bench. 'I'm already set.' She didn't wait for an answer, just headed for the fridge. She thought it best to keep busy, keep that whimpering to an absolute minimum. Water, wine, she grabbed both and set them in front of him. 'Help yourself.'

He did, reaching for a couple of tumblers on the shelf nearby before pouring water for them both. He snagged another glass, a wineglass this time, and filled that too, his fingers long and lean around the neck of the bottle…fingers that looked as if they could deliver anything a woman could possibly want, from a feather-light stroke to firm and knowing pressure in all the right places.

'There it goes again,' he said. 'That sound.'

'Could be the tabby cat hereabouts. She's very noisy.'

Pete looked at the curled and sleeping cat over in the corner of the kitchen, her head firmly tucked beneath one paw. 'You mean *that* cat?'

'Yes.' She said it with an utterly straight face and Pete's admiration for her rose immeasurably. 'That cat.'

They ate from the picnic table in the courtyard, with the cottage nestled into the hillside behind them and the sea spread out before them like a promise.

'So how many brothers do you have?' Pete asked between bites of truly divine roast chicken. Chicken like this could quite conceivably make a man change his mind on the issue of not wanting a woman to come home to each night.

Serena held up two fingers and he smiled. Two brothers and an overprotective cousin wasn't so bad.

'I saw that smile,' she said darkly. 'And if you figure you can handle them you're wrong. They're half Greek. And if you're talking extended family—and with my family you should—I also have two brothers-in-law, a father, three uncles, and half a dozen male cousins my age or older. Nico is the most liberal-minded of the lot.'

'Ah.' That was quite a list of protective males. Doubtless she'd driven them insane during her teenage years. 'Bet your first date went well.'

'You have no idea,' she muttered. 'I thought he'd be all right. He had a very cool car and a bad-boy reputation. A smile that promised heaven… They were waiting for him out in the front yard when he came to pick me up. My father and my uncle.' Her eyes flashed with a mixture of amusement and annoyance. 'They'd brought home a fish from the morning's catch and were gutting it when he pulled up. With ten inch boning knives.'

'Sounds reasonable,' said Pete. 'Although I can see how you might consider the knives a touch melodramatic.'

'It was a six-foot shark.'

'Oh.' He felt a smile coming on.

'And don't you dare laugh!'

'No, ma'am. But I am impressed.'

'We didn't even get to the cinema. The poor boy took me to a burger drive-through, fed me hot chips and a sundae, and had me home within half an hour. He's probably still running.'

'Just for the record, I'd have bought you a burger as well.' He topped up her wineglass, reached for another slice of bread. 'I have three brothers, a father, and one sister. Hallie's the youngest.'

'No mother?'

'Nope. She died when I was a kid. My father took it hard, pulled back. My brothers and I took over the raising of Hallie. You'd like her. You could swap stories. My youngest brother could get downright creative when it came to deterring her more persistent suitors. He works for Interpol these days. He'd have *loved* a shark as a prop.'

'Are you sure you don't have any Greek ancestry in you?'

'Not a drop.'

'What's your position on trust and honour?'

'As in Nico trusting me not to hit on you?'

She nodded.

'It's damn near killing me.'

Her smile sliced through him, wicked with challenge. 'But you *are* sticking to it.'

'Barely.' The meal had more than satisfied Pete's appetite for food, and dusk was warming up the crowd for the coming of night. The air lay heavy with the scent of jasmine and he was self-aware enough to know that if he didn't leave soon his honour wouldn't be worth a drachma. 'Close your eyes,' he told her. 'Think back to that bad boy with his own car and a smile like a promise.'

'Why?' But she did as he asked, her back to the table, her elbows resting behind her, and her head tilted back a fraction as if to catch the moonlight.

'Work with me here,' he murmured. 'You've been to the cinema and you're on your way home. The car stereo's blaring, the windows are down, the wind is in your hair, and your bad boy has forgotten all about your father's shark-carving skills. He's young and reckless, and so are you.'

Her lips curved. 'And then?'

'He pulls up outside your front yard.'

'Does he stop the engine?'

'No. He's not insane. He's planning on a quick getaway.'

Her eyes were still closed. 'Where's the shark?'

'Your father and uncle are hauling the last of it into the freezer. The timing's perfect.'

'For what?' she whispered.

'This.' He brushed his lips over hers, a fleeting touch, nothing more, and pulled away. He planned to end it then, to say goodnight and get the hell out of temptation's way, but her eyes were still closed and before he knew it his lips were on hers again, questing, cajoling, because this time, *this* time he wanted a response.

He got one.

Serena had played his game because she wanted to. Because she was curious as to what this man with his come to bed eyes and go to hell grin could bring to an evening, a moment, a kiss.

He brought plenty.

A taste so wild and delicious she shuddered. A mouth so firm and knowing she responded instinctively, following his lead with lips and with tongue in a dance as old as time. She wanted more, slid her hand to his cheek, to the nape of his neck in search of it, taking the kiss deeper as she sought the recklessness in him, that piece of him that courted danger, revelled in it, and came back for more. She found it.

And the kiss turned wild.

He murmured something, a deep-chested rumble that sounded like a protest but felt like surrender, and took her under.

Her mind had clouded over by the time the kiss ended, the rapid pulsing of her blood at odds with the languid slide of her hand from around his neck. She leaned back, elbows on the table, and watched as he struggled to surface, clawing his way out of the kiss in much the same way she had, and not bothering to hide how hard he found it.

She liked that about him. She liked it a lot.

'Damn but he's gonna break some hearts, kissing like that,' she murmured.

'So are you.'

She made a small hum of pleasure. 'Tell him to kiss me again.'

'No. If he does he'll be lost and he doesn't want that. Besides, the porch light has just come on and it's way past time to be leaving.'

'Does he come back?'

'Try keeping him away. It's your first kiss, maybe his third, but from that moment on there's a part of him that'll always be yours.'

She smiled, enchanted by his whimsy.

'Thank you for the meal,' he said softly. 'Serena?'

'What?'

'I'll honour Nico's trust in me tonight, but next time I see you I'll be asking you out to dinner. I'll be holding you at the end of the evening. I'll be around these next few weeks. I'll be taking up some of your free time.'

She liked his high-handedness. She liked it a lot.

'And Serena?' He stood and looked down at her, looking for all the world like a dark angel fallen straight from the sky. 'I don't give a damn how big the shark is.'

CHAPTER THREE

PETE BENNETT lived to fly. Nothing could change that. Nothing ever had. It was simple fact that he was at his happiest with one hand on the throttle and the other on the joystick of a helicopter that responded to his slightest touch. Oh, he had his favourites, everyone did, and luckily old Tomas's Jet Ranger was one of them. She was no Seahawk—equipment-wise she was a purely civilian fit—but she had a light touch and he was close to the sea, and for now that was enough.

And if at times skimming low across the water put him in mind of other far more dangerous flights and missions, well, that couldn't be helped. A man like him did his damnedest to ignore the insistent knocking of the past in favour of whatever else was in front of him.

A man like him took great pains to ensure that whatever was in front of him had a certain basic appeal.

Island-hopping with a cargo of two tourists looking to overnight on a sleepy Greek island, for example, had enough basic appeal in the shape of meeting up with Serena again to drive every unwanted memory from his body.

He touched down at Sathi, Varanissi's picturesque seaport, just on three in the afternoon, unloaded his passengers, and herded them towards the hotel, their bags slung over his shoulder with his own.

The fiery Chloe was nowhere to be seen as he saw them checked in and arranged to meet them again at nine the following morning. He wasn't as lucky when it came to the boy, Sam. The kid had appeared in the foyer as he'd arrived and had been hovering ever since. When Pete made to leave, young Sam ventured forward.

'You're not staying here?' he said.

Pete shook his head. 'I'm staying up at Nico's. In Tomas's room.'

'Oh.' Sam paused, as if weighing his options. 'I'm heading up that way too. To see Nico. I could show you a short cut if you want.'

He knew the path the boy was talking about. He'd taken it before, with Nico. And opened his mouth to say so.

But Sam had already read him. Pete watched, eyes narrowing, as bleak resignation flashed across the kid's face, just before he lifted his chin and looked away. How the hell did a kid get to be so streetwise and still be so soft? He didn't know. But it got to him. 'Fine,' he said, perversely pleased by Sam's surprise. 'I figured I'd head on up to the Vespas and say hello to Serena after that. Join me if you want. I could use the company.' This much was true. He'd be far less tempted to reach for Serena within moments of seeing her if he had Sam with him.

Given the wildness of his fantasies about her, that was probably a good thing.

* * *

Four days. Four endless summer days. That was how long Serena had been waiting for that damn helicopter to fly over and land on the island and even then she waited another hour for the pilot of the cursed machine to put in an appearance at her brand-new blue beach umbrella by the rusty Vespa shed. By that time Serena had replayed the memory of Pete Bennett's kisses at least a thousand times and every cell in her body was screaming for more. The man was a genius.

But he wasn't alone. Sam tagged alongside him, wary and silent but nonetheless there. So much for wrapping herself around Superman right then and there.

Make that evil genius.

'Hey, sailor,' she said, smiling at Sam who'd finagled a morning out on Nico's boat tomorrow. Tomorrow being Saturday, and that being the deal he'd made with Chloe if he went to school all week. 'Got a message for you. Nico said he'll swing by on his way down to the dock at around four-thirty a.m. Speaking from experience, you'd better be ready because the tide waits for no man and neither does Nico. Wear a jumper and a hat and don't worry about gloves. He's found some for you that'll fit.'

Serena watched as Sam's face lit up like the sun, a fleeting grin, gone almost as soon as it had arrived but she'd caught it nonetheless, along with a hefty dose of hero-worship for her cousin. 'Meanwhile, there's a Vespa been coughing and spluttering and I need someone to take it around the paddock a few times to see if it gives any grief.'

'What's in it for me?' said Sam.

'Experience,' she said dryly, handing him a helmet.

'It just so happens that the bike you'll be trialling could well be the second-fastest bike on the island.'

'So Aunt Chloe went for it?' asked Pete as they watched Sam fasten the helmet, start the bike and ride slowly along the fence line. '*That's* the second-fastest bike on the island?'

'Well, no. Not any more. Maybe thirty years ago.' Right now, it was the slowest ride she had. 'And Chloe caved two days ago after two more trips to the principal's office on account of our friend here's somewhat disquieting habit of disappearing from school around mid-morning and failing to return.' The bike coped with the downhill run easily enough, but coughed and groaned all the way up the hill. 'I think it needs a new spark plug.'

'That or a decent burial,' muttered Pete.

'We don't discard our old around here. It's just not done,' she told him. 'And it's about time you showed up.'

Pete Bennett smiled. 'Miss me?'

'Maybe. Did *you* miss me?'

'Of course. How many goddesses of buckets and sensuality do you think I know?'

'Pardon?'

'Never mind. I tried to get back here earlier,' he murmured. 'Unfortunately, not many people know about this place. It's a hard sell. Maybe you should hurry up with those postcards.'

'Maybe I will.' She eyed his carryall speculatively, wondering how Sam had found him so fast, wondering exactly how long he was staying this time. 'Are you staying overnight?'

He nodded. 'What time do you finish up here?'

'The last of the bikes should be back by five, give or take half an hour,' she told him. 'Why? What did you have in mind?'

'I'm thinking of taking a stroll up the hill.'

'What hill?' She followed his gaze to the mountain looming behind them. 'Oh. That hill.' She'd climbed it before. It wasn't easy. 'That's a big hill.'

'Sam says there's a path to the top.'

'Well, yes. There is. If you're a goat.'

'And that you can see the entire island when you get to the top.'

There was that.

'Bring your camera. You might catch the sunset.'

She'd been here for five months, four days, and counting. She'd photographed *everything* more times than she cared to remember, including the sunset. 'I'll need more incentive than that.'

'It's good exercise.'

'Boy, do you have a lot to learn about women and incentive.'

'C'mon, Rena. Haven't you ever wanted to touch the sky?'

He had the soul of a poet. The smile of a devil. Serena couldn't resist either. 'All right. I give in. We'll walk to the top and touch the sky.'

His smile promised more, much, *much* more, and she knew for a fact he could deliver. 'You won't regret it,' he murmured.

'I never do.'

* * *

It was half past five before the last of the bikes were locked away for the night and Serena had shooed Sam home. Closer to six by the time they'd taken her cooler and the cashbox down to the cottage. There was enough daylight left for getting up the hill. Not nearly enough daylight for getting back down. Serena picked up a small canvas bag and went in search of a torch and a couple of bottles of water before slinging it over her shoulder. 'Ready?'

With a gesture that came as automatically to him as breathing, Pete removed the bag from her shoulder and slung it over his. 'Lead on.'

She led him behind the cottage and across the bitumen road to where the goat track began. If there was one thing she'd become used to on Varanissi, it was walking up hills. Her body had grown quite fond of it; her legs no longer gave protest. She was healthy. Fit. And still she had the feeling that if necessary, Pete Bennett with his lazy stride and easy breathing could have taken the slope at a dead run. She picked up the pace, figuring that if she had to exercise she might as well make it worthwhile.

Half an hour later they reached their destination, a desolate plateau dropping away sharply on three of its four sides, but what the rocky, barren plateau lacked in visual appeal it more than made up for with its panoramic view of the village and harbour below.

The island had charm; she'd give it that. And the people on it were as good as you'd find anywhere. Maybe better.

But the world was bigger than this, and so were

Serena's dreams. Pete Bennett knew how to dream big too. She could see it in the way he looked to the sky, sense the restlessness in him, a burning need to keep moving, keep going…to run, and to fly. 'You love it, don't you? Being up here.'

'Yeah,' he said simply, looking skyward. 'It's the next best thing to being up there.'

'Why helicopters?' she asked. 'Why didn't you choose to fly planes?'

'I've flown both,' he said. 'But helicopters are more sensitive, more tactile machines than planes. Planes are all about power. Helicopters are about finesse.'

'You fly planes too?'

He flashed her a grin. 'Serena, I fly everything.'

'Have you always wanted to fly?'

'Ever since I was old enough to sit on my sainted mother's knee at Richmond RAAF base and watch the pilots practise their touch and gos.'

'I'll take that as an always. What's a touch and go?'

'You bring the plane in, touch down, and then take off again, all in the same run. What about you?' He gestured towards the camera around her neck. 'Has it always been photography for you?'

'Not always. I've done lots of things. Managed restaurants, designed their interiors, done the branding work for the family seafood outlets, written articles for magazines. But I keep coming back to my camera and the stories a picture can tell.' She took a mouthful of water. Watched as Pete did the same, slaking his thirst the same way he'd climbed the hill: effortlessly and with every appearance of enjoyment. 'So you spent a goodly portion of your childhood hanging over the fence of the local RAAF base. What then? How did you become a pilot?'

'I was all set to join the Air Force but somewhere along the way I got to stand on a deck full of Navy Seahawks and that was it for me. Nothing else would do.'

'You joined the Navy?' It didn't seem to fit with his carefree bad-boy image. 'What about the discipline? All those rules and regulations? Dedication to duty?'

'What about them?' He shot her a quizzical glance.

She figured she might as well give it to him straight. 'You don't seem the type.'

'Look harder,' he offered, his voice noticeably cooler.

Good idea. Excellent idea. She slipped the cap from her camera and studied him through the lens. 'Okay, I'm seeing it now.' But only because he was letting her see. This was a part of himself that playboy Pete Bennett preferred to keep hidden. She took the shot, and then another. 'So how long were you in the Navy?'

'Regular squadron? Seven years.'

'And then?'

'Then I transferred to air-sea search and rescue helicopters for a while.'

'For how long?' There was something about his expression that didn't invite questions.

'Eight years.'

He looked away, all shut down, but not before she'd caught with her camera a hint of pain that ran deep. She wondered at it, wondered why a man who'd spent fifteen years in service to others was currently flying tourists around these islands and contemplating hauling cargo around PNG. A man didn't walk away from the kind of work he'd been doing for no reason. Did he? 'Do you miss it?'

'Miss what?'

'The howling winds and heaving seas. The adrenalin rush that'd come with battling the elements and saving lives. It's pretty heroic stuff.'

'I'm not a hero, Serena. Far from it. Paint me as one and you'll be in for disappointment,' he said quietly.

'Thanks for the warning,' she countered dryly. 'You know, my father is a fourth-generation fisherman. My brothers are fishermen. My cousins are fishermen. I *know* who they look to for miracles when the sea turns ugly and a vessel goes down. I know what you used to do.'

'I don't do it any more.' The reckless charmer had disappeared, and in his place stood a complex warrior. The rogue had been irresistible enough. The warrior was downright breathtaking. 'Take your photos,' he said, but she already had and they wouldn't be appearing on any picture postcard.

'C'mere,' she said softly and he looked towards her, wary and wounded for reasons she couldn't fathom, his dark glare daring her to probe and prod for answers he didn't want to give only she was done with questions for now. First rule of interviewing was to read your mark and when you'd pushed them as far as they'd go, pull back and come at them later from a different direction.

He stepped up in front of her, big and brooding, his hands in his pockets and his expression guarded. 'Closer,' she said, and set her hand to his chest and lightly bussed his lips. 'That's for stepping up to protect your country—even if you were seduced into it by a bunch of Navy helicopters.' She set her lips to his again and let them linger a fraction longer, watching as his eyes darkened. 'And that's for putting your life on the line to save others, day in, day out, for eight years.' She slid her hand to his shoulder and this time her kiss was more than a whisper. She felt his response, saw with satisfaction the heat of the kiss chase the shadows from his eyes.

'What was that for?' he muttered.

'Dinner,' she said, sauntering away towards the southern edge of the plateau. 'You *are* taking me to dinner, aren't you?'

He took her to dinner. To the little restaurant high in the hills where the fish stew was reputed to taste like ambrosia and the air was thin enough to have him breathing deep whenever Serena looked at him. She wore a cream-coloured dress, low cut, square necked, with delicate shoulder straps. It had little buttons all the way down the front, buttons that drove a man to distraction whenever he looked at them, and she knew it, her smile told him so and her eyes dared him to call her on it. 'That's quite a first-date dress.' His lips brushed her hair as he saw her seated. 'But it's not blue.'

'You were expecting the blue?' she said and her eyes were laughing.

'I was looking forward to it,' he said. 'With a great deal of anticipation, I might add.'

'Sorry to disappoint.'

'You haven't. I'll continue to look forward to it.'

'I'm saving it,' she said.

'For what?'

'The Trevi Fountain.'

Good call. He knew this game of seduction well. He loved the playing of it, the hunt and the chase. Loved it when his quarry provided a challenge. And heaven help him the woman sitting opposite knew exactly how to do just that.

'Unfortunately my chances of venturing that far afield are somewhat limited at the moment,' she added with a sigh. 'And I suspect you're tied to Tomas's charter operation as well. Fortunately for you I've had another idea.' She leaned back in her chair and smiled. 'It involves no fountain and no blue dress whatsoever, but it does involve water.' He was all ears. And damned if she didn't smile and change the subject. 'Tell me about your family.'

'I've already told you about them,' he said.

'Tell me more.'

He usually didn't. But this time, in this place, he relaxed into his seat and offered up more. 'My father lives in Sydney. He's an academic—a scholar of ancient Chinese pottery. My sister is married and lives in London. She inherited our father's passion for pots. Then there's Tristan, who works for Interpol. He got married at Christmas and is back living in Sydney.' Pete shook his head at the wonder of that particular notion. 'Then there's Luke. He's older than Tris, younger than me. He's a Navy SEAL.' Pete toyed with his bread and butter knife, would have left it at that, but Serena wasn't chasing a career in photojournalism without having mastered the finer art of persistence.

'You said you had three brothers,' she prompted him with a smile. 'There's one more.'

'Jake.' Thoughts of Jake always came with a serve of guilt. That he hadn't helped him out more when their mother had died. That he hadn't shouldered more of the responsibility. 'He's a couple of years older than me and runs a handful of martial arts dojos in Singapore.'

'So your family is scattered all over the globe.'

'More or less.'

'My immediate family live in Melbourne. All of them. I can't imagine them living anywhere but in each other's pockets.'

'Is this a bad thing?' he asked curiously.

'Hard to say.' She shrugged. 'Everyone always knows what everyone else is doing. Whether that's a bad thing tends to depend on whether they approve of what you're doing. If they don't…' She shrugged again.

'And do your family approve of your plans for the future? The photojournalism career? The endless travel away from the family bosom?'

'Let's just say they don't quite understand,' she said lightly, but her eyes told a different, darker story.

'Maybe one day they will.'

She smiled and leaned back in her chair. 'You're a nice man, Pete Bennett. Idealistic, but nice.'

There was that word again. Nice. She really should stop bandying it about. It made a man uncomfortable. 'You do know that *nice* isn't really on this evening's agenda?' he told her softly. 'That would be the wrong notion to be carrying around altogether.'

Her smile held equal measures of wickedness and delight. 'I'd be very disappointed if it was.'

A weathered old man appeared beside the table, glaring at him from beneath thick grey eyebrows and over a strongly hooked nose. 'You'll order now,' he said.

Pete looked to Serena and raised an eyebrow. 'Care to order?'

'My usual, Pappou Theo. The fish stew and the salad.'

'*Pappou* Theo?' he murmured.

'Honorary grandfather,' she said. 'One of my grandfather's pinochle partners.'

That explained the scowl. 'I'll have the oysters and then the fish stew,' he said. 'Serena tells me good things about it.'

'No oysters for you!' said the old man emphatically. 'Greek salad with many onions. You'll like.' The old man turned to Serena again and surveyed her critically. 'Does Nico know you're here?'

'Yes, Pappou.'

'And when does he expect you home? At a reasonable hour, I hope.'

'Yes, Pappou. Very reasonable.'

The old man muttered to himself beneath his breath and turned back to Pete. 'Drinks?' he barked.

'Some white wine?' Pete looked to Serena.

'No!' said the old man. 'No wine.'

'Raki?'

'Pig swill,' he said.

'Beer?'

'Not for you. I'll bring the water over,' said the old man, and stalked away.

Pete stared after him. 'That went well.'

'I did warn you,' she said. 'I *told* you there'd be sharks. You told *me* you could swim.'

'I can swim.' And he was enjoying the challenge of getting past her guardians. He watched as the old man ambled towards the kitchen with their order. 'I'm just rethinking our next evening meal. I have a plan.'

'Is it a cunning plan?'

'It involves travel off the island. For you.'

'I like it,' she said. 'Simple yet effective.'

'How far away do you think we'll have to get before you run out of relatives?'

'Three or four islands over,' she said breezily. 'Five at the most. Or we could play it really safe and go to Istanbul for the evening. That'd work.'

'You don't have any relatives in Turkey?'

'None we admit to.'

'So…' He began to think of more immediate options. 'What would a man have to do to earn your family's approval to court you?'

'You want to court me? I'm thinking courtship comes under the heading of *nice* again.'

'I'm speaking theoretically.'

'Well, theoretically, it'd help if you were Greek and owned a shipping line.'

'How about Australian and co-owner of a small charter airline?'

'I'd have to check. Tell me…are you of Greek Orthodox religion?'

'Catholic,' he said with a shrug. 'Lapsed.'

'You might want to keep that to yourself,' she said.

'You should probably stick to talk of undying devotion to me, an exceptionally large income, a huge wedding, and your longing to help produce half a dozen children in very short order.'

'*How* many children?' he spluttered.

'Oh, okay, five then. But that's my absolute minimum.'

'You want *five* children? In very short order? Are we *sure* about this?' She didn't look all that sure. 'Two,' he said firmly. 'Two's a good number. Any more than two and we won't all fit in the helicopter.'

'Four,' she countered with a grin. 'And we're definitely going to need a bigger helicopter. Something roomy and safe. Family-minded. A Volvo of a helicopter.'

'Oh, that's harsh,' he murmured. 'Anyone would think you didn't *want* a man to consider a serious relationship with you.'

'They'd be right.'

'God, you're perfect,' he said. 'I swear you stand a very good chance of ruining me for all other women.'

'That's quite a compliment,' she countered. 'But I really don't want to ruin you for anyone. I just want to play a while.'

'Utterly and irrevocably perfect,' he said on a sigh. 'Hell, Serena, you might just ruin me anyway.'

Their meal arrived and they ate it. Sinfully rich stew with a smattering of easy conversation on the side. Pete knew the game of seduction very well and played it with a skill that left her breathless and more than a little intrigued as to what would come next. A rakish smile or a challenging question? A sidestep here, advance, or retreat? He kept her guessing. Kept her amused and entertained.

She was a curious woman by nature, but he did a remarkable job of making her want to know more of him. Like what it was that had put the shadows in his eyes, and what he was doing here, flying tourists around the sky, when every instinct she owned told her there was so much more to him than this.

'Coffee?' he suggested as Theo cleared their plates away. 'Dessert?' Theo opened his mouth as if to refuse them that as well. Pete eyed him coolly. 'Of course, if there's nothing available here I'd be happy to take you somewhere else.'

They got their coffee and dessert. They also got a taxi without having to order it. It was leaving within the next five minutes, Theo told them. It'd be a good idea if Serena were in it. She didn't disagree.

Pete looked amused but neither did he.

They were back at the little whitewashed cottage on the hillside by a quarter to ten. Serena waited in silence as Pete paid the taxi driver and, stepping back, looked towards her front door. 'No sharks,' he said. 'There's a surprise.'

'Nico's pretty easygoing,' she said dryly. 'I can't see him objecting too much to our having dinner up at Theo's.'

'Can't you?' There was that soul-stealing smile again. 'I can.'

Nico had left the outside light on for them, but before she could decide how to end the evening, whether to invite him in, cut and run, or try and figure out something in between, the door opened and Nico stood there glaring at them both.

'You're still awake,' she said, surprised. Nico usually bedded down far earlier than this. All that getting-up-before-dawn business.

'Have you *any* idea how many phone calls I've had about you tonight?' he demanded.

'Er…more than you wanted?'

'One was more than I wanted. I've had four. Four! Two from Theo, one from Marianne Papadopoulos, and one from your mother! And don't ask me how she knew you were out on a date, because I have no idea. Anyone would think you were making love on the tabletop.' He eyed them narrowly. 'Were you?'

'No!' Serena's hands went to her hips and her temper slid up a notch. 'We were *trying* to have a meal, and a restricted one at that. When was the last time *you* went out to dinner and Theo refused you oysters and alcohol?'

Nico's lips twitched.

Serena narrowed her eyes. 'Don't you dare laugh.'

'Not laughing,' he said, and then spoiled it by grinning hugely as he turned away and stalked back down the hall. 'This isn't Australia,' he said over his shoulder. 'It isn't even Athens. What did you expect?' He spared a lightning glance for Pete. 'You've got five minutes. I need my sleep. Anything happens to Sam on board that boat tomorrow and Chloe'll skewer me with a fish-hook. Anything happens to Serena in the next five minutes that's not entirely circumspect and I'll skewer you. That's the way it works around here. Welcome to Sathi.'

'All right,' she said with a sigh as she closed the door on Nico's retreating form and turning to study the man at her side. 'So I could have been *slightly* wrong about Nico not worrying about our dinner together—although, to be scrupulously fair, he probably wasn't the one doing the worrying. Others did it for him. How do you feel? Alarmed? Afraid? Threatened?'

'Nah.' Far from looking worried, Superman looked to be thoroughly enjoying himself. 'He gave me five minutes. He likes me.'

She liked him. And that was proving more of a problem than she'd thought it would be. 'Walk with me, Pete Bennett. I'll show you my favourite place in the garden.' She clasped her arms around her waist and walked around the side of the cottage, to the edge of the garden to stare out over the moonlit sea. She did some of her best thinking just sitting there staring out to sea.

She needed to do some very serious thinking about what she wanted from this man right about now.

She'd looked at him a few days back and seen a pleasant diversion. A charming playmate with no strings attached. She looked at him now and saw something far more dangerous. A man with a generous heart, and a guarded one. A man with the potential to captivate her as well as charm her, and she didn't want that. No, she couldn't have that.

Not when for the first time in her life she could see a time up ahead with no commitments and no family ties. *Her* time. Time for chasing long-held dreams for a career she could be proud of.

'I've enjoyed your company,' Serena said at last.

Nothing but the truth in that statement. 'I'd like to enjoy it some more. But we're going to need some rules.'

'I love rules,' he said. 'What kind of rules?'

'We keep this light-hearted,' she said firmly. 'No falling in love.'

'Check.'

'And brief. We'll both be leaving here soon enough. We should make that the end of it. Clean break. Happy memories.'

'Mature of us,' he said. 'Anything else?'

'I know we're talking a brief and in no way serious relationship here, but I'm thinking exclusivity is a must.'

'You'd better be,' he said curtly.

'There *is* one more thing.'

'You're pushing your luck, Serena.'

He looked tough, forbidding, and Serena wondered afresh whether she was insane to think she could handle this man. He walked his own path, made his own rules. But this last rule was important. 'We need to be discreet.' Otherwise it would reflect badly on her family, and she didn't want that. 'It's this place…' she said with more than a little frustration.

Pete laughed at that, and the rich dark sound of it slid along her skin like water.

'You're right,' he murmured. 'We'll be discreet.' And then his lips were on hers, hard and seeking, and all her carefully thought out rules shattered beneath the weight of her desire.

Pete's body betrayed him the moment he reached for her. He'd known it would. The searing heat. The outrageous, all-consuming need to possess that which he held and, in doing so, offer up a part of himself. She was all luscious curves, made for a man's hands, *his* hands, as he curled his fingers around her buttocks and brought their lower bodies into languid and intimate contact. He could be discreet. If that was what she wanted. He'd do it. He would.

Soon.

Just as soon as he'd finished feasting on her mouth.

She dug her hands in his hair and her lips turned ravenous, but he was ready for the staggering hunger of her kisses this time and he ate them up, spun them round, and served them straight back at her.

Serena had thought she was prepared for the passion this man brought to lovemaking, but she wasn't prepared for this. It was like a meeting of souls, locked in a kiss, and she feared it…heaven help her she feared it…even as she gloried in it. Whatever she wanted, however she wanted it, he had it in him to give. And she wanted it all.

Shuddering at the sensations threatening to overwhelm her, she dragged her lips free of his kiss and set trembling fingers to his mouth instead. A barrier, a slowdown, only her fingers had a mind of their own, exploring his upper lip, the strong shapely curve of it, before dragging the sensitive pad of her forefinger across the sculpted fullness of the rest.

Serena watched as those perfect lips curved into a smile; a smile for her attempts to regain control maybe; and then she was urging his mouth open and replacing fingertips with lips and with tongue for a kiss so staggeringly potent she clear forgot to breathe.

Whatever she wanted, she thought helplessly as his

tongue duelled delicately with hers. Just the way she wanted it, as his fingers tightened on her butt and he surged against her, and with a ragged groan spun them into the maelstrom again.

His eyes were black, as black as sin and deep enough to drown in, when finally, finally, they stood apart.

'Discreet.' He ran a hand around the back of his neck. 'We might have to work on that one,' he said raggedly. And then he was gone.

CHAPTER FOUR

NICO scowled at her when she staggered into the kitchen. Serena ignored him and headed for the sink, filling a tall glass to the brim with tap water and downing it in one long swallow. 'So…' she said, finally turning to face her cousin. 'How was your night?'

Nico's eyes narrowed. 'I *said* five minutes.'

'It *was* five minutes.'

'It was ten minutes, your mouth's all swollen, and your hands are shaking.'

Oh.

'You can't take a man like that seriously, Serena.'

'I don't intend to.'

'I mean, what do we know about him? Apart from the fact that he was able to pack up his life in an instant and come out here when Tomas called. Seriously, what does that say about a man?'

'That he's a good friend to Tomas?'

'He's a drifter. A man with no responsibilities.'

'You should ask him what he used to do for a living,' she said wryly. 'It's quite illuminating.'

'He's trouble. I thought you could handle him or I'd never have introduced you.'

'I *can* handle him,' she snapped. She'd had enough of Nico's and everyone else's well-meaning interference. 'I know damn well he's trouble. I don't need you to tell me that. I know it wouldn't work out. I don't *want* it to work out. All right?' Her voice broke but the rest of her stood tall as she glared across the table at Nico and dared him to take her to task for a passion she couldn't control. 'I know.'

Pete was fresh out of a cold shower in the little bedsit, a towel slung around his waist and his hair still dripping water, when he took it in his head to call his older brother. In Singapore.

''Lo.' Jake's voice sounded raspy, sleepy.

'Jake? What time is it there?' He did the maths, winced a little at the early morning hour. 'I, ah, didn't interrupt anything, did I?'

'Not unless you count sleep as something. Which you should.'

'Never mind. I'll call back later.'

'You in trouble?' asked Jake.

'Not really.'

Jake said nothing. Jake was really good at waiting in silence while the other person squirmed and tried to put feelings into words. Something to do with inner stillness and meditation. He'd never quite managed to get the hang of it, himself. 'All right, so I could have a *slight* problem.'

'Define "slight".'

'There's this woman.'

Dead silence at that. Fraught silence. Not a lot of inner stillness in that silence at all. And then, 'Why me?' said Jake, his voice long-suffering. 'I live a frugal life. I keep to myself. I pay my taxes… Why?'

'Is this a bad time to call?' he said. 'Because I can call back later. When you're making more sense.'

'Is she terminally ill?'

'No.'

'Are *you* terminally ill?'

'No.'

'Is she married to a Mafia Don who wants to cut off your balls?'

'She's not married at all.'

'So there's no bodily danger to you at this particular point in time?'

'No.' It was his soul he was worried about. 'My body thinks it's found heaven.'

'Colour me envious,' said Jake, 'but what the *hell* is your problem?'

'She doesn't want to be tied down.'

'So? Neither do you. The minute a woman starts getting serious, you're gone.'

'This one's kind of interesting.'

Silence.

'You've fallen for her,' said Jake finally.

'I have not!' he said indignantly. 'I did *not* say that. I was just wondering what the next step up from a strictly casual relationship might be. You know…casual yet slightly meaningful. Comes before commitment. But I can't remember what it's called.'

'Self-delusion,' said Jake dryly. 'Run.'

'That's your advice? Run?'

'Yep.'

'Any *other* advice?'

'Nope.'

'You are no help whatsoever.'

'Not in this,' said Jake with grim humour. 'Call Tris,' he said, and hung up.

No way, thought Pete as he shoved the phone back in his bag. No way was he calling *anyone* else in his family tonight. One delusional phone call an evening was enough. He towelled his hair, found a fresh pair of boxers in his carryall and looked at the bed.

He was nowhere near ready for bed.

He found a book, tossed it on the bed as incentive.

Still not ready for bed. The image of a dark-eyed goddess in an ivory-coloured sundress flashed through his mind, closely followed by an image of her lying in his bed with no ivory-coloured sundress on at all.

Now he'd *never* get to sleep.

So she wanted nothing more than a light hearted romp. Was this a bad thing? No. Light hearted romps were his speciality.

So he'd wondered, *briefly*, about a relationship that involved a little bit...more. Clearly not a good idea. He'd get over it. *Was* over it. A short-term relationship was fine. Just fine.

Fidelity he could do.

As for discretion... Pete thought back to the kisses they'd shared and chuckled as he stripped the towel from his body and ran it over his hair.

Heaven help them both.

* * *

Breakfast the following morning was a revelation. Serena had rapped on the bedsit door at seven and told him that breakfast was available in the kitchen if he wanted it. Ten minutes later he made his way over there, showered, shaved and ready for whatever lay ahead as far as light hearted, short-term, discreetly exclusive relationships were concerned.

And then he stepped through the kitchen doorway and she stopped grinding fresh coffee beans and smiled at him and every rational thought he'd had about her left his head.

She wore modest shorts and a bright pink T-shirt— Pete recognised it as her Vespa hire attire—and had pulled her hair back into a pony-tail. Nothing overtly seductive about any of it—no slinky sleepwear or artfully tousled hair, and still her innate sensuality punched into him like a fist.

'What would you like for breakfast?' she asked as she loaded up the breakfast bench with far more food than he could possibly eat.

'You don't have to do this, you know,' he said as he relieved her of the orange juice and gestured towards the bench. 'I can get my own cereal.'

'All part of the service.' She stifled a yawn and padded over to the kitchen sink, leaning over to open the window above it. 'You want anything cooked? Sausages? Bacon and eggs?'

What he *wanted* was to drag her back to bed and make love to her until the sleepiness left her eyes and satisfaction took its place. What he *wanted* was to ask her what she had planned for the day and then rearrange his own schedule to fit in around hers so he could see her again later. What he *said* was, 'No, thanks. This is fine.'

'So…' she poured herself a cup of coffee and cradled it in her hands as she leaned back against the kitchen counter and studied him '…what do you usually talk about at breakfast?'

'Usually I'm by myself.'

'When you're not,' she said dryly.

He tried to think. Couldn't. Not when she strolled over and settled into the chair opposite him and her scent wrapped around him like a promise. 'Work. We talk about work. What that person is doing with their day. That sort of thing. '

'Oh,' she said. And with another one of those lazy, loaded smiles, 'What are you doing with your day, Pete Bennett?'

'Well…' He wished his mind would return from wherever he'd dropped it. It was probably somewhere over by the door. 'First up is Corfu to drop passengers, then Cyprus to pick up some cargo, then back to mainland Greece. I'll overnight in Athens.'

'Skite,' she muttered. '*I'm* going to the Vespa shed. I'll be there until five.'

'I'll think of you.' Nothing but the truth.

'What else do you talk about?'

'Anything. Everything. Except for home improvements. A woman starts talking home improvements and I start to get nervous.'

'Really?' she said archly. 'So you don't think this kitchen needs a bigger window? I think it needs a much bigger window. I mean, look at that view! It's just begging to be taken advantage of.'

'It doesn't work when you talk about improvements to *your* home,' he told her smugly as he reached for the cereal. 'It only works when the house in question is *mine*.'

'Ah. I should have guessed.'

'You should be grateful,' he told her. 'You don't *want* a man who's looking for a woman to improve his home, remember?'

'Not yet, anyway,' she murmured.

'So…you *do* want one eventually?' This was interesting.

'Well, yes,' she said with a toss of her head. 'Eventually. But now is not convenient.'

'Why not?'

'I want to travel for a while. Concentrate on my career. Be free of family for a bit. Family commitments are messy. They confuse things.'

'So…you're streamlining.' Pete looked around at the mass of food, remembering the easy way she dealt with Nico and with Sam, with everyone who crossed her path, and stifled a grin.

Serena's eyes narrowed. 'Something amusing you?'

'If I had to hazard a guess I'd say you *liked* life a little messy and complicated.'

'Maybe in the past,' she said. 'Maybe for another few *weeks*. But in a month's time life is going to be sleek, career-focussed, and ever so slightly narcissistic.'

'Hence our rules for this relationship.'

'Exactly. I knew you'd understand. More coffee?'

Pete kept his expression deadpan as she breezed her

way through the breakfast ritual. Toast, animated discussion of a story in the newspaper, a grocery list for Nico... He ate his cereal, watched her put a load of Nico's work clothes in the washing machine, and wondered afresh at humankind's capacity for self-delusion. The fresh-brewed-coffee goddess didn't have a narcissistic bone in her body. Oh, she might have looked the part, but beneath all that blatant sensuality lay an innate regard for the welfare of others that he doubted she'd ever shake.

No matter what kind of plans she'd made for the future.

His watch told him it was time to fly. His stomach told him there was no reason to linger over breakfast any longer. Sighing, Pete stood and took his breakfast bowl and coffee-cup over to the sink.

'You're right. You do need a bigger window here,' he said as she came to stand beside him.

'I knew you'd see it my way.' Serena smiled and leaned back against the counter, her hands either side of her as he stepped in closer, effectively trapping her between himself and the counter. Her smile widened.

'Maybe instead of dinner next time, we could do something your honorary protectors don't object to quite so much. We could go sightseeing.' He brushed her lips with his. 'Swimming.' Another kiss, just as fleeting. 'Something.'

'When will you be back this way?' she murmured, leaning towards him and lifting her mouth towards his for a kiss rich with promise and in no way fleeting. His mind had fogged and he was a whisper away from taking things further when finally she drew away.

'Soon.'

Just over one week later, Serena sat at the desk in her grandparents' tiny sitting room that doubled as an office and waded through her latest batch of job applications. She'd commandeered one of Nico's fishing crew to run the Vespa hire business for the afternoon so she could get this latest lot done and on their way. Trouble was, she was doing more daydreaming than working and her pile of completed job applications didn't seem to be getting any bigger. Time was wasting. Flying.

Wrong word. Serena scowled and tried very hard not to think of other things that might be flying, a particular *person* who might be flying for example, although he certainly hadn't been flying *her* way of late.

He'd *said* he'd be back soon. One week did not qualify as *soon*.

When it came to life on the island, one week bore a startling resemblance to eternity.

'Nico said I'd find you here,' said a deep voice from the doorway and Serena caught her breath at the sudden rapid pounding of her heart. She turned slowly, her brain wrestling her wayward body for control of her next actions. Her body was all for launching itself into his arms and getting frantic fast. Her brain wanted something a little more demure and nonchalant. Something composed.

She settled for leaning back in her chair and swirling round to face him, chin high in silent defiance of the effect he had on her body. She could control this. She could. 'You're late,' she said darkly, drinking him in, those startling good looks, the smile in his eyes and the way his lips tilted at her words.

'How goes the job hunting?' he said.

'It's probably best if you don't ask about the job hunting right now.'

'That bad, huh?'

'Let's just say there's not a lot here that makes my heart go pitter patter.' Apart from the obvious.

'So can I persuade you to take some time out to go for a Vespa ride or a swim?'

With a smile like that he could doubtless persuade her to do *anything*. Not that he needed to know that.

'I can probably spare a few hours. Distractions aren't all that common around here. When they arrive we tend to make time for them. It's just the island way.' There. Nonchalant had been well and truly nailed. Who said she had no control around this man? She looked at the carryall at his feet. 'Are you staying overnight?'

'Two hours.'

'That's *it*?' Her nonchalance headed south, never mind the nails.

'I have a pick-up in Santorini later this afternoon. Business is booming.'

Bummer. She stacked her papers into a pile and shut down her laptop. Two hours was still two hours. No point wasting it. 'I hope you have a towel in your bag. And swimmers.'

'Happens I do,' he said.

Hers were in her room. 'I'll meet you in the courtyard in three minutes. Help yourself to some food from the kitchen on the way.'

Three minutes later she stood by the fastest Vespa on the island—which wasn't saying much—with Superman beside her munching an apple as she contemplated their next step. 'What would you rather do first? Swim or sightsee? There's a good swimming cove nearby. Some pretty little churches up in the hills. Do you like churches?'

'They have their uses. But I'd rather swim first and repent later,' he said with a decidedly unangelic smile.

'I like your thinking.' Such a good catholic. She looked at the Vespa, looked back at Pete. 'Who's driving?'

His lips twitched as his gaze met hers. 'Now there's a question.'

'I'm the one who knows where we're going,' she said reasonably.

'True,' he said with a sigh, shoving his hands in his pockets and staring dejectedly at the bike for good measure. 'There's no arguing with that.'

Serena rolled her eyes at the pitiful image of male self sacrifice before her. 'Or we could go past the shed and get another Vespa. Then we could both be in the driver's seat.'

'A marginally better idea,' he said. 'If you discount the wasted fuel.'

They stared at the bike some more.

'You could always give me directions,' he said.

'Can you *take* directions?' she asked sceptically.

'Why wouldn't I?'

'There doesn't need to be a *reason*.' Clearly he'd never been in the car with her parents.

'Not only can I take directions, I also have an equal

opportunity plan of attack for this particular dilemma,' he said. 'Me being a thoroughly modern man and all.'

Serena snorted. 'Let's hear it, then.' He wasn't quite as traditional in his thinking as her father and brothers when it came to womenfolk and their place in the world. But he wasn't that far off it.

'I'll drive us to the beach, you can drive us to the church,' he said with a grin. 'We'll start tossing coins after that.'

'My hero.' Wonders would never cease.

He handed her his carry bag and straddled the bike. She slung the bag over her shoulder, next to her own, and slipped onto the bike, her hands at his waist and her sundress riding high on her thighs so that when she settled into place behind him her bare thighs nudged the lightweight cotton material of his trousers and the tightly muscled buttocks beneath. Maybe there was something to be said for not being in the driver's seat after all. This was very nice. Very…liberating. Perfect, in fact.

But wait. She'd wrinkled his shirt and she couldn't have that. So she let her hands roam all over that wide muscled back; a wrinkle smoothed here, a wrinkle made there. Really, there was just no getting rid of them.

'Serena—' His voice was husky, more than a little strained.

'Hmm?'

'What *are* you doing?'

'Ironing.'

'Well, can you do it later?' he muttered. 'I'm trying to concentrate here.'

'Oh.' She slid her hands beneath his shirt and set them to his waist, set her feet to the footpegs, her knees tucking in behind his and bringing her thighs into even closer contact with the back of his. 'Sorry. Ready when you are.'

'Serena—' He sounded long suffering, his voice a deep delicious rumble that started in his chest and carried all the way to the tips of her fingers as well as her ears. There was just no *end* to the sensory delights to be found on the back of this bike. 'The directions—'

'Oh. Right.' Serena grinned as he started the bike. 'Turn left and drive. The road follows the coastline. I'll tell you when we're there.'

'That's it?' he said. 'Those are the directions?'

'They're good, aren't they?' she said and settled back to enjoy the ride.

Serena took him to a secluded cove with white sand, clear blue water and a swimming cave she knew damn well he'd want to explore. Sure enough his eyes lit up when he saw it and he wasted no time stripping down to his board shorts. He wore clothes well, no denying it. But he wore next to no clothes better. He was all lean and sculpted muscle, not an ounce of fat on him. Sheer perfection, but for a thin, wicked-looking scar that started high on his back and headed up and over his left shoulder.

She stepped closer and traced its path with gentle fingers. 'What's this?'

'A reminder,' he said gruffly. 'And you're underdressed.'

She took care of that, stripping down to her bikini before rummaging through her shoulder bag for some sunscreen. She smoothed it over her shoulders and down her arms, noting with some satisfaction that she'd managed to divert his attention from the cave. She slid her hand behind her hair and lifted it forward, over her shoulder, and handed him the sunscreen before presenting her all but bare back to him. 'Do you mind?' she murmured. She wanted his hands on her. She wanted her hands on him. She'd been dreaming of it.

Pete stood back and surveyed the vision splendid in front of him with the appreciative eye of a true connoisseur. So many curves, all of them lethal. And they were his for the coating. Pete tried to remember when life had last been this good...

Nope. Nothing.

Life had *never* been this good.

'Nice day for a swim,' said a voice beside him, and he turned his head to find an elderly Greek woman standing beside him wearing a scary black one-piece swim suit. Sturdy body. Thighs. And a white bathing cap covered in plastic yellow flowers. 'Marianne Papadopoulos,' she said briskly. 'I run the local bakery. We haven't met.'

Serena tilted her head, one hand still holding the bulk of her hair. 'Hello Mrs Papadopoulos.' Serena sounded amused. Resigned. 'This is Pete Bennett. He's filling in for Tomas. But you probably already know that.'

'Of course,' said Marianne, deftly removing the sunscreen from Pete's grasp and squirting a generous amount into her palm before sending the bottle of sunscreen over Serena's shoulder and tapping her none too gently with it.

'Thanks.' Serena's voice was dry, very dry, as she reached up to take it back.

'You can't be too careful about sun damage these days,' said Marianne, rubbing her hands together before slapping them down onto Serena's back and moving them about with vigour. White streaks began to form; a criss-cross of streaks on a canvas of glorious golden skin. Picasso would have been impressed. Pete wasn't so much impressed as resigned. They really did need to get off this island and onto another one.

Tahiti sounded nice.

'Will you be staying overnight?' asked Marianne.

'No, ma'am,' he told her politely. 'I'm only here for a couple of hours.'

'Just enough time for a swim and maybe a trip up into the hills before we head back to Sathi,' said Serena, turning round and squaring up to Marianne Papadopoulos with admirable aplomb.

But Marianne was undeterred. 'I noticed you only brought one bike,' she said.

'Pete's very fuel-conscious,' countered Serena. 'For a pilot.'

'You should take two bikes next time. Your grandfather would not mind.' She looked meaningfully towards him and Pete stifled the urge to reach for his clothes and start pulling them on. 'Your grandfather would prefer it.'

'I might just…swim,' he said, seeking escape, finding a likely avenue in the crystal-clear water of the cove.

'Good idea,' said Marianne. 'Swim. Cool off. I'll come too. It's not good to swim alone.' And she headed majestically towards the water.

'Another one of your grandfather's pinochle partners?' he muttered.

'Uh-huh.'

'Frightening.'

'You have no idea.'

'Maybe I'll just swim on over to the cave and *you* can swim with Marianne.' Sharks he could handle. White bathing caps with plastic yellow flowers were *way* beyond his sphere of experience.

'Leave me alone with her and you're a dead man,' she muttered.

Pete contemplated his options. There was really nothing for it but to take Serena with him. He grabbed her hand and raced towards the water, Serena giggling helplessly as they sped past their latest chaperon, kicking up spray as feet met water, before finally getting far enough into the water to plunge beneath it.

He surfaced a fair way out, with Serena right beside him, and turned back towards Marianne, who clearly preferred a more leisurely entry into the water. 'We're just heading over to the cave. We'll be right back.'

Marianne's hands went to her hips. Pete grinned and set off for the cave at a fast crawl with Serena matching him all the way, agile as a seal and just as sleek.

'I'm ruined,' she said with a reckless smile.

'But you haven't done anything,' he argued. Nor had he. Yet.

'You're right.' She gave Marianne a wave. 'Maybe I'm only partially ruined. If we stay within her sight and you stay, oh…' she gestured about a body length's distance with her hands '…about this far away from me, we might even manage discreet.'

Oh, yeah. Discreet. Vaguely platonic. He'd forgotten about that. 'Do we *need* to manage discreet?' he queried. 'Is it really essential?'

'This is Sathi,' she said. 'It's a necessity.'

So he played by the rules and they dived for shells in the shallows and stayed within sight of Marianne and finally swum back to her and floated about and made small talk about the various sights to be seen on the island. By the time they left the water and had dried off an hour had passed and there was no time left for sightseeing anyway.

'I'd better be heading back.' He slung his towel in his carryall, watched with a sigh as Serena slung a dress over all those glorious curves and twisted her hair back into a pony-tail.

'You can drive,' she said, picking up her carry bag and heading across the sand towards the bike.

'Are you sure?' he said, deftly catching her bag and slinging it over his own shoulder. He didn't much like riding shotgun but he'd said he'd do it. Fair was fair.

'Very sure. Go ahead.' A tiny smile played about her lips. 'I insist.'

Three days later, Serena sat on the little beach at the water's edge, paintbrush in hand as she touched up the name on her grandfather's prize fishing boat. Not changed it, mind. The name of a fishing boat *never* changed once it had been bestowed, but touch-ups were allowed, and the free flowing black scrawl was sorely in need of it. The boat was called *Plenty*, and Serena was trying very hard to convince herself that that was exactly what she had.

Nico had decided that she needed another break from the Vespas and had organised one of his fishing crew to cover for her for the day, so one thing she had was plenty of time. He'd convinced her to come down to the beach beside the fishing-boat docks and repaint the name on the boat while he rolled out the nets and set to repairing holes. Sam had found them not long after they'd beached the boat, Chloe had found them not long after that, but instead of ordering Sam home she'd sat down and started repairing the holes in the net too, with a deftness that spoke of previous experience. Technically, thought Serena, she had plenty of company.

In just under two weeks her stint on the island would be up and she'd be free to do whatever she wanted.

Plenty to think about there.

It was a crying shame that the only thing she *had* been thinking about lately was a laughing, complicated man with the smile of a rogue, the soul of an eagle, and a heart that seemed to beat in time with her own.

'Fool,' she muttered.

'There she goes again,' said Sam, looking up from his inspection of the net and shooting Nico one of those man-to-man looks. 'Talking to herself.'

'Let it be a lesson to you, Sam,' murmured Nico. 'Wear a hat.'

'How do you know I'm not talking to you?' she said to Nico, reloading her brush with paint before spearing him with a dark glare. 'It's possible. Extremely possible.'

Nico rolled his eyes at Sam. Sam grinned back. 'I saw that,' she said darkly.

'She's been twitchy for days,' continued Nico with a sigh. 'Moody. Some might even say pining. One might even hazard a guess as to what she's been pining *for*.'

'Oh, good. A man with a death wish,' she said with a toss of her head. 'And I am *not* pining for anything. I'm just…contemplating the universe.'

And then a helicopter appeared on the horizon where sea met sky, heading towards them low and fast.

'Look! It's Pete,' said Sam, and Nico sniggered.

The chopper drew closer. Close enough for Serena to see Pete and two passengers. Sam leapt to his feet and waved. Chloe waved too. Even Nico looked up and grinned.

Serena gritted her teeth and turned her attention back to the Greek word for *Plenty*.

'Can I go see if he's staying over?' asked Sam as the chopper headed for the landing pad behind the hotel. 'He might want to come and mend nets too.'

'*If* he's staying,' she muttered. 'Sometimes he doesn't.' Sometimes he just dropped by to torture her.

'If he is staying he'll probably be after a room at the hotel,' Nico told Chloe.

'You banished him?' said Chloe.

'You *banished* him?' demanded Serena.

'Had to,' he said. 'By order of Marianne and Theo. They fear for your virtue.'

'Quite right,' said Chloe. 'A girl can't be too careful. Not on this island. You have no idea how people gossip.'

'We went *swimming*,' said Serena. 'That's *all* we did.'

'That's not what I heard,' said Chloe dryly. 'Marianne had to save you from total ravishment at the cove. She got there just in time. One second later and he'd have had his hands all over you. That's her story and she's sticking to it.'

'It's a good story,' said Serena with a wistful sigh. 'I even vaguely recognise some parts of it.' She turned to Nico and eyed him narrowly. 'Exactly *when* did you banish him?'

'The day you went swimming,' he said amiably. 'I phoned him and explained the situation and he offered to bunk down at the hotel straight away. Said he had his reputation to think about. And yours. Mentioned the word discreet a few times. Mentioned something about a whale shark and a yellow-flowered bathing cap.' Nico shuddered. 'I didn't want to know.'

Serena sniggered.

'So he's staying at the hotel?' Sam asked Nico, his eyes bright.

Nico nodded. 'Most probably.'

Sam took off across the beach with an unguarded enthusiasm Serena envied, only to halt abruptly some ten metres away. Serena watched as he turned back, not towards her or Nico this time, but towards Chloe. It was the first time he'd paid her the slightest attention all morning. 'What room can we give him?' he asked her. 'The big one? Number seventeen?'

'Provided no one's in it,' she said, looking up at him from her spot on the sand, her hands full of fishing net as she considered his question. 'Otherwise he can have number two. That's another one we sometimes use for upgrades. Tell Reception to put it through at the discount rate.'

Sam left at a run and Chloe watched him go, her face alight with happiness. 'Did you hear that?' she said in wonder. 'Sam said *we*. As in him and me. He didn't even think about it. He just said it.'

'You give the pilot your best room?' demanded Nico. 'At a discount rate? For what?'

'I like him,' she said, pleasure easing to puzzlement.

Nico glared at her.

Serena glared at her too.

'Well, I do,' she said defensively. 'He's nice to Sam. He talks up the hotel to his passengers…'

'Yeah, but what else do you know about him?' muttered Nico.

Chloe's eyes took on a decidedly teasing gleam. 'He's handsome, polite—?

'Almost penniless, not Greek, a lapsed Catholic…' added Serena, although the penniless bit was probably a stretch. Not if he co-owned an air-charter business. 'And, oh, yeah, he's running from something. Don't forget to factor that in.'

'How romantic.' Chloe slid her a sideways glance. 'What do you think he's running from? A tragedy? A world full of injustice? A woman?'

'A life of crime?' muttered Nico. 'Come on, Chloe.

He's not a saint. He flies tourists around the sky, for heaven's sake.'

'And before that, he used to fly air-sea rescue helicopters,' said Serena.

Nico stared at her in silence. So did Chloe.

'All right,' her cousin said finally. 'So he hasn't always been a penniless drifter. That's quite a job. Some women might even think it sounds romantic—although they'd be *wrong*.' He glared at Chloe. 'But can he fish?'

CHAPTER FIVE

PETE was five steps from the front door of Chloe's hotel, his duffel slung over his shoulder and his mind on a dark-eyed goddess he'd promised to court discreetly, when Sam hightailed it past him to hold the door open for him before making a beeline for the reception desk. The passengers Pete had flown to the island were staying with family, he had no need to help anyone else check in, no one else's belongings but his own to carry, no one to answer to until mid-morning the following day. Nothing to do but suit himself.

As far as Pete was concerned, suiting himself involved checking in, grabbing something to eat at some stage, and finding Serena.

Furious whispering ensued as he headed towards the desk. Maybe they were booked out? Maybe that was what all the fuss was about? Because, without question, they were fussing about something. Sam beamed. The receptionist blushed.

'Checking in, sir?' she said. 'Do you have a booking?'

'Not yet. I'm after a room for the night. If you have one.'

'Certainly, sir. One person?'

Pete nodded.

'You'll be in room seventeen.'

He handed over his credit card and she processed his payment and handed him a key. 'Enjoy your stay.'

'You want me to carry your bag?' asked Sam.

'Why? You working here now too?'

'Nope.' Sam paused as if to consider the notion, his eyes brightening. 'Not yet. But I could. Do you think she'd pay me?'

'Who? Your Aunt Chloe? Maybe.' He studied the boy. 'You need money?'

'Doesn't everyone?'

'What for?'

'Stuff.'

'What kind of stuff?'

The boy shrugged. 'Just stuff.'

Pete opened the door to room seventeen and looked around. 'Nice room,' he said.

Sam's smile broadened.

Pete dumped his duffel on the end of the bed and deliberately turned to survey the minibar. 'Do you drink, Sam?'

Sam's mouth set into a thin stubborn line. 'No.'

'Smoke?'

'No.'

'Shoot?'

'I *said* no!'

'Good for you,' he said mildly. 'Then why are you so determined to start work and earn money?'

Sam didn't answer him, just stood silently in the doorway with a stubborn set to his jaw that Pete was more than familiar with having grown up in a household full of siblings who were anything but malleable. He held Sam's gaze and waited, not stern, not demanding, just waiting. Borrowing the technique from Jake—hell, it always seemed to work for *him*.

'What if I need to buy food, or shoes?' said Sam abruptly. 'What if I need to buy medicine for—' The boy stopped, looking as stricken as Pete suddenly felt. 'What if I get sick?' he said in a small, thin voice.

'Your family will take care of that kind of stuff for you, Sam,' he said gruffly.

'And if they don't?'

'They will. Your aunt Chloe will.'

There was a world of mistrust in Sam's eyes. 'You don't know that.'

'You're right, I don't.' He'd lost his mother, just like Sam. But he'd never been alone. He'd always had his brothers to rely on. Even when their father had fallen apart, he'd always had his siblings. Sam had had no one and Pete couldn't begin to imagine what the boy had gone through—was still going through if his dogged determination to work and to earn his own way was any indication. 'But I'll bet you fifty euros that if you get sick your aunt will get you the medicine, or the doctors, or the hospital care you need.' He fished his wallet from his pocket, withdrew a fifty euro-note and tossed it down on the bed. He withdrew another note. 'I'll bet you another fifty she'll never let you go hungry.'

Sam stared at him with those dark, haunted eyes. Wanting to believe, thought Pete. Desperately wanting it to be so, when experience had only ever taught him otherwise. 'I don't have a hundred euros to bet with,' Sam said at last.

'You don't need it. If your aunt lets you down the money's yours. If she doesn't, you give it back. That's the deal,' he said, but still the boy hesitated. 'Take it or leave it.' Pete turned away, started to unpack his duffel. When he turned back Sam was standing by the bed and the money was gone.

'Deal,' said Sam awkwardly.

Pete nodded. Maybe with some money in his pocket the kid would feel slightly more secure. He hoped so.

'Everyone's down at the beach fixing nets,' Sam said next. 'You could come down too.'

'I have a few things to do here first.' He was trying to be discreet. Trying very hard not to go looking for Serena the minute he set foot on the island. Although... Maybe seeing her now was *better* than seeing her later. Maybe being seen with her openly, in the company of others, was the epitome of discreet in Sathi. Who knew?

Sam studied him curiously. 'Serena's down there.'

'So I saw.'

'She keeps talking to herself. Nico reckons she's pining for something.'

'Does he now?'

'Yeah. Serena reckons Nico's got a death wish.'

'Maybe I will come down,' he said, stifling a grin. After all, Sam *had* come looking for him. Nico and Serena and Chloe had to be thinking it was okay for him to join them otherwise they wouldn't have let Sam come looking for him in the first place. Right?

Besides, denial wasn't exactly one of his strong suites.

What Pete Bennett wanted, he usually got.

Fast.

Serena had decided to be cool, calm, and in control if the flying one decided to join them down on the beach. Cool was a shoe in given that she was wearing short white shorts, a pink and lime bikini top, and currently stood knee deep in water. Calm and in control were proving a little more problematic given that her heart was hammering and her brain had chosen to replay the beach kiss scene in *From Here To Eternity* and suggest it as a viable greeting option.

'*Not!*' she muttered vehemently and glared at Nico when he laughed.

Maybe if she'd had a little more forewarning she might have been able to manage calm and in control. Honestly, couldn't he have called ahead to let her know he'd be flying in?

Didn't the man know how to use a *phone*?

On the other hand, maybe he wasn't even stopping, just dropping passengers and flying on. That was possible too.

Not that she cared if he stayed or if he left. No. He was a distraction, nothing more, and distractions could always be replaced by other distractions.

Trying to paint signage while scanning the waterfront walkway every few seconds, for example, was very distracting.

She botched the curve of the middle letter about the same time she spotted Pete and Sam heading towards the beach from the direction of the village. Not the most direct route from the hotel by any stretch of the imagination, but the reason for their detour could probably be explained by the newspaper Pete carried in one hand, and the woven blue and white shopping bag he carried in the other. The reason for her botched paint job probably had something to do with the way he filled out a white crew-necked T-shirt and an old pair of cargo trousers cut off at the knee.

'There they are,' said Chloe.

'Mmm.' She was trying for an indifferent-sounding 'mmm,' but figured from Chloe's smirk that it had emerged as a whimper. Hopefully Chloe would think she was staring at the shopping bag.

Pete took his own sweet time making his way down to the boat. He stopped to kick off his shoes when he reached the sand. Stopped again to share a few words with a couple of elderly tourists.

When he stopped with Sam to poke at a mound of seaweed and watch a tiny soldier crab scuttle back into its hole in the sand she could have screamed.

He knew *exactly* what he was doing to her. Making her wait. And want. And want some more.

Damn but he was good at this game.

'Serena,' said Pete with a nod, when he and Sam finally reached her. He leaned into the boat and set the shopping bag and the papers inside it before sending her a lazy, non-committal smile, but it wasn't enough. She wanted more. Exactly how much more currently being a subject of much internal debate between her body and her brain.

'Hey, flyboy.' She was *not* changing her plans for him.

'Apple and honey cake?' he said affably.

She was going to become a successful international photojournalist! She didn't *want* to be a suburban housewife. 'No,' she snapped, before reconsidering the question actually on the table. 'Yes.' She jammed the paintbrush back into its pot. 'Thank you.'

'You're welcome.' He eyed her warily. 'Something wrong?'

'It's this island,' she muttered.

'She needs to get off it,' said Nico, zeroing in on that woven shopping bag like a seagull after a crust. Chloe wasn't far behind him. Not that she blamed them. Marianne Papadopoulos might have been the biggest gossip on the island, but her pastries could make grizzled Greek fisherman get down on their knees and beg. The woven shopping bag Pete had carried down to the boat was one of the ones she saved for special treats and Nico knew it. 'What's in the bag?'

'Apple and honey cake,' she said. 'And it's for *me*.'

'Actually, I bought it for all of us,' said Pete. 'I *would* have bought something just for you but I'm being discreet.'

'Makes sense to me,' said Nico, delving into the bag. 'Look, she even sliced it for us. Who's the big bit for?'

'Sam,' said Pete. 'As directed by Mrs Papadopoulos herself.'

'She likes you, Sam,' said Chloe, eyeing the slice. 'That's a *big* bit of cake.'

Sam looked at the cake, looked at Chloe. 'You can have it if you like,' he offered awkwardly. 'I'm not that hungry.'

Chloe stared at him in startled silence, Nico smiled, and Pete turned away but not before Serena caught the hefty dose of concern in his eyes. Serena didn't know what was going on. But it felt big.

'Thank you, Sam, but I couldn't. I'd never hear the end of it,' said Chloe, trying to make light of his unexpected gesture and not quite managing it. Her eyes were too bright. Her voice wobbled too much. 'It's yours.' She reached into the box and selected a smaller piece. 'Save it for later if you don't feel like eating it now.'

Later, by Sam's reckoning, turned out to be approximately two seconds later. He took the cake and, head down, went back to examining the nets for holes. Loading themselves up in similar fashion, Nico and Pete did the same.

'I should have taken it, shouldn't I?' whispered Chloe anxiously, her gaze still on Sam. 'He offered, and I turned it down. I did it all wrong.'

'No.' Serena laid a hand on the other woman's arm. 'It's okay, you did fine. It was sweet of Sam to offer, and right of you to turn it down.' Her thoughts turned to Nico and to what she as a good and helpful cousin might do to support his cause. 'Of course, if you wanted to capitalise on the whole food sharing business you'd go over there and very casually offer to help Sam cook up the sea bass he caught this morning, and even more casually suggest that Nico come over later and help you eat it.'

Chloe blushed furiously, her eyes wide and panicked as she turned back to Serena. 'But, Serena, I couldn't! That would put Nico in a terrible position. It'd be almost like a *date* or something.'

'What if it was? Would that be so bad?' Serena shook

her head. 'Get to know my cousin, Chloe. You might be surprised.'

'I don't *want* to be surprised! Nico will leave here soon. They always leave.' She shrugged and looked back towards the village. 'Whereas me…I couldn't leave here even if I wanted to. My parents are old. Someone has to run the hotel. That someone is me. I have to make good, especially now I have Sam.'

'You know from my point of view Nico's leaving here is somewhat negotiable,' said Serena, after a moment. 'He could make this place his home, given the right incentive. Look at him showing Sam how to roll the nets. He *likes* fishing. He likes being a part of this community. He likes *you.*'

Chloe stayed silent, but her gaze skittered back to Nico and Sam. She was scared of opening herself up to hurt, Serena got that. But surely she could see that in this case the prize was well worth the risk? 'So if you like *him*, maybe you need to think about giving the man a reason to stay.'

Serena ate apple and honey cake while Chloe headed up the beach towards the nets and Pete headed back down the beach towards her. They stopped midway to chat, while Serena brushed the crumbs from her hands and wet sand from her legs and tried to remember how she was supposed to be acting around this man. Cool, calm and collected, that was it.

Definitely a stretch.

But he made it easy for her as he made small talk about the island and his charter customers, settling back against the boat and leafing through the newspapers he'd brought with him. *The Times* was one of them; *The Australian* was the other one.

'I saw a job in here for you earlier,' he said as he reached into the cake box for another slice of cake. Serena eyed it wistfully. If she had any more of that cake she'd be up for some serious exercise afterwards. Tempting…but no. 'They're looking for a political foreign correspondent. It's based in Jerusalem though.'

'I could do Jerusalem.'

'Can you do Hebrew?'

'Do I need to?'

'Beats me.' He pulled out the jobs section and passed it to her. 'Keep it.'

She waded the few feet to the shore and set her paint pot down, pushing it into the wet sand to stop it from spilling before settling down beside it and opening up the paper. Nothing like a world of possibilities to distract her from a vision sublime of man and cake, both of which she wanted far more than common sense allowed.

'There's one in here for you too,' she said after a few minutes of silent browsing. 'Feel like flying climate-control scientists around Greenland?'

'No.'

'Why not?'

'Because I'd freeze. Here's another one.' He'd been leafing through *The Australian*. 'They're looking for a Wilderness Society photographer. This one's based in Tasmania.'

'You think I have environmentalist tendencies?'

'Serena, you're trying to send me to *Greenland*.'

Good point. 'Tasmania might be a little too close to home,' she told him. 'I'm thinking further afield.' Pete glanced at her and shook his head. Serena lifted her chin. She knew that look. Usually it preceded a lecture about setting goals that were realistic, not to mention closer to home. 'What? You think I'm wrong to want my freedom?'

'I think you should be choosing your future career based on the work you'll be doing and whether it'll satisfy you, not on how far away it is from your family.'

Another good point.

'You'll miss them, you know.' He wasn't looking at her. He was looking at Sam, thinking of Sam, unless she missed her guess. 'You don't know how lucky you are to have a family who cares for you. People you can rely on because they love you.'

'He's talked to you, hasn't he?'

Pete looked at her but said nothing.

'Sam. He's talked to you. About his mother.'

'No.'

'About Chloe, then? And not fitting in here.'

'No.' And at her look of disbelief, 'What?'

Honestly, men! They had no idea how to communicate. 'Well, what *did* you talk about?'

'Money, and stuff.'

Serena sighed heavily and shook her head. '*Talk* to him next time. See if you can get him to open up to you about his feelings.'

Pete snorted. 'Not gonna happen, Serena.'

'Why not?'

'Because it won't.' He glanced back at Sam. 'He's doing okay.'

Serena followed his gaze to where Sam and Nico sat mending the net. She narrowed her eyes, automatically framing the shot as she waded out into the water and reached for the camera she'd tucked inside the boat. The pattern of the nets contrasted with the ripples in the sand beneath and presented an interesting juxtaposition, but it was the focus both Nico and Sam brought to their task that interested her. The wordless connection between them as boy looked to man for guidance. Nico's nod of approval; the pleasure and quiet pride Sam took in it... She captured every heart wrenching nuance, and knew instinctively that somewhere amongst the photos she'd just taken she'd find the final image for her postcard series and that it could well be the best photo she'd ever taken.

'Here, grab a brush and let's get this done,' she said to Pete, picking up the paint pot and handing it to him. 'We're getting out of here.'

'We are?' He took the paint pot with the brush sticking out of it and wandered around to the bow of the boat to survey her work. 'I only just got here.'

'How do you feel about spending the afternoon working on postcard photos?'

'Do I have a choice?'

'No. You'll like it. Trust me.'

'Does it involve a darkroom?' He smiled a pirate's smile. 'I love darkrooms.'

'Excellent,' she said. 'Start painting.'

'I thought you said you had a darkroom,' Pete muttered half an hour later. They were up at her grandparents' little whitewashed cottage, in a neat little sitting room that looked as if it doubled as an office. A widescreen laptop computer sat on a table in the corner beside a printer. Half a dozen folders stood beside that. There was nothing wrong with it, as far as rooms went. But it wasn't quite what he'd had in mind. 'You know, dark, private, *discreet.*'

'I said no such thing,' Serena said cheerfully and pulled down the window shades, switched on the computer, and sat down in front of it. 'You just *assumed* we'd need a darkroom. Welcome to the age of digital photography. The days of broom-cupboard darkrooms and messy, smelly chemicals are long gone.'

Pity. He'd had a fantasy or two about broom cupboards, beautiful women, and the mingling thereof. Guess it'd have to stay a fantasy. 'These photos had better be good,' he said with a sigh as he pulled up a chair and settled down beside her to watch her work.

The photos were better than good. They were outstanding. From a wide-angle shot of Mrs Papadopoulos watering the geraniums out the front of her shop to the latest shot of Nico and Sam, they showed the power of the human spirit, with all its strengths and frailties.

'Forget the words, Serena,' he told her bluntly. 'Your pictures don't need them.'

'There's another one you might like to see,' she said after a moment. 'It's not for the postcard series, though.'

'What's it for, then?'

'You.' She trawled through her files until she found it. Pete sat back in his chair, aiming for distance, and wished to hell she hadn't. It was one of the photos she'd taken of him when they were up on the plateau. She'd captured his solitude, he thought, trying to be objective. And she'd captured a pain he'd thought he'd buried deep.

'If I were a curious woman,' she said with a tiny half-smile, 'I'd ask you what you were thinking about.'

'If I were the sharing kind I'd tell you.' He glanced away; he didn't want to look at his picture any longer. One day he'd stop running. He'd turn and face his past and all that went with it. Maybe one day he'd even make his peace with it. But not today.

'No great tragedy?'

'No,' he muttered as she stood and pushed the laptop aside before leaning her backside on the table, curling her hands around the edge of the table, and regarding him solemnly. 'You're very persistent, aren't you?'

'So I'm told.'

Not that it seemed to bother her.

'*Something* put that look in your eyes,' she said at last.

'Experience.' He spanned her waist with his hands and slid her towards him in one effortless movement. She was still perched on the edge of the table. He still sat in the chair. Their bodies weren't quite touching, not yet, but if…when…he pulled her into his lap she'd be straddling him. 'Nothing more, nothing less.' His hands were rough, her stomach was silky smooth and just begging to be kissed. He slid her closer and set to tracing lazy circles across her stomach with his fingertips, before leaning back in the chair and glancing up at her face to gauge her reaction.

If the flush of colour riding high on her cheeks and the lip she'd caught between her teeth were any indication, she liked his hands on her just fine. So did he. 'I went into air-sea rescue battle-trained and ready for anything,' he said wryly. 'Or so I thought.'

'Cocky,' she murmured as her hands settled on his shoulders. 'Invincible.'

'Yeah. And when you save a soul that would have been lost that's exactly how you feel.' He didn't know why he was telling her this. He should stop now, leave it be, but her eyes didn't judge him and the hands on his shoulders were warm and somehow soothing, and he offered up more. 'It's the best feeling in the world. The best *job* in the world. But when you don't…' He paused and drew in a long breath before continuing. 'They take a little piece of you with them.'

Somewhere along the way he'd stopped tracing circles on her skin. He started up again, slower this time, lower, until they scraped the waistband of her shorts. 'Got that way there wasn't much of me left. Got that way that the person I needed to save most was me. I couldn't do it any more, Serena. So I left.' He leaned back in the chair, concentrating on the present, on those little white shorts, and the woman in his arms. *Hell* of a way to woo her, he thought with a twist of his lips. *Hell* of a way to make her think well of him.

'You think you've failed them, don't you? The people who trained you? The people you couldn't save?'

'I did fail them.'

'Don't be so hard on yourself,' she said quietly. 'No one gets to save them all. Not even Superman.'

'You believe in Superman?' He tried for a smile and

almost managed it. Enough soul-baring. Enough. He couldn't do this.

'I believe in you.'

'Oh, hell, Serena.' He drew her closer, wrapping his arms around her waist and resting his forehead on her stomach. 'Don't.'

'Too late.' She wound her hands in his hair and drew his head back before sliding from the table and into his lap as if she belonged there, as if she'd always belonged there. His body responded instantly, even if his brain was still playing catch-up. He felt himself harden beneath her slight weight, inhaled the essence of her and the scent of the sea, and shuddered.

'You know what you need?' she said lightly. 'Right this very moment?'

'A change of subject,' he said curtly. No question.

'Comfort.' She shifted, and those little white shorts she wore shifted right along with her, all softness and warmth against his growing hardness. 'Lucky for you I give good comfort.'

But it wasn't comfort that he wanted from her. 'What about distraction?' Because she was way off on the comfort angle. Way off. 'Do you provide that too?'

'Mmm hmm.' She set her lips to his earlobe and her hands slid from his shoulders to his waist and then lower, stopping only to create havoc beneath the hem of his T-shirt. 'I think you'll find me an excellent distraction.'

And then her lips were on his, teasing, giving, and the world and his struggle to find a place in it disappeared beneath the weight of his desire for her. His passion built and so did his urge to bury himself deep inside her; to take and take still more, until the only name he remembered was hers.

He tried to damp it down. He called on every last bit of skill he possessed to keep things simple and easy between them, just as she wanted. Just as he'd always been able to do with a woman before. With words and with every drop of control he'd ever been taught, he tried to delay the inevitable. 'I'm still waiting on that blue dress,' he told her raggedly as he twined a strand of her hair, that midnight-dark hair, around his finger, around his fist.

'Maybe if you'd told me you were *coming*,' she countered as she slid his T-shirt heavenward.

He helped her take it off, dropping it on the floor beside him before reaching for her again, finding the curve of her throat with his lips as he surged against her, heat to heat, centre to hard, unyielding centre. 'Trust me, Serena. I guarantee you'll know when I'm coming.'

He watched her face as he traced a path from the hollow of her throat, down over the curve of her breasts with his fingers, smiling his satisfaction when her eyes grew slumberous and her nipples peaked for him beneath the slippery material of her bikini top. 'Distract me some more,' he murmured, leaning back in the chair, still trying for lightness between them, and her smile turned impish.

'You're a beautiful man, Pete Bennett,' she said as she leaned back and lifted her hand to the bikini tie at the back of her neck, sliding it forward so that it lay on the curve of her breast. 'Sculpted enough to make a woman sigh her gratitude. Hard enough to make her tremble in anticipation.' She toyed with the end of that string, back and forth, back and forth, until his fingers twined with hers and he took over that particular duty.

He tugged on it gently, not enough to loosen it altogether, not yet, and she shuddered and bit back a whimper, playing the game he'd asked of her, playing it to perfection. He *could* have tugged that string loose completely and covered the tightly peaked nubs of her nipples with his mouth but he wasn't quite ready to give up his sanity just yet.

He smoothed his hands over those golden shoulders, played his hands along her arms until his hands found hers and he set them palm to palm, smiling a little at the contrast. She had beautiful hands, smooth, feminine. A direct contrast to his much larger, rougher hands, and one that pleased him. She studied their joined hands with a tilt to her lips that told her the contrast amused her too, and then she threaded her fingers through his and made his hands prisoners.

'You'd rather I didn't touch you?' he queried as her lips traced a path from his jaw to the edge of his mouth. 'That's a pity.'

'I *do* want you to touch me,' she assured him. 'Soon. Very soon. But it's *very* distracting and that's not good, because right now *I'm* the one who's doing the distracting.'

'You're right. You're absolutely right,' he murmured, closing his fingers over hers. 'But you'll let me know when you're done with that?'

'Of course.' Her lips met his for a kiss so deeply drugging that he groaned beneath the onslaught.

'Are you done yet?' he demanded raggedly.

'No.' Another kiss followed, more potent than the first.

'How about now?'

'Patience, flyboy.' But she punctuated her remark by loosening her grasp on his hands as she arched back, her body undulating ever so gently against his—like the lapping of the tide—and any patience he might have laid claim to disappeared beneath a wave of exquisite pleasure.

His hands left hers to slide over her skin, over her belly button, over the thin cotton material of those little white shorts, as he played his knuckles across the area just above where his body met hers. Back and forth, back and forth, while his body demanded more.

'I think I'm done distracting you,' she whispered.

'You're sure?'

She looked down to where his hand played over those little white shorts and shuddered hard against him, all feminine strength and outrageous heat. 'Positive.'

'Because I'd hate to rush you.'

Her eyes met his, dark and needy, as her fingers found her bikini string and tugged it loose. 'You're not.'

Her breasts were full and round, dusky tipped and perfect, and fitted his hands as if they belonged there. She gasped, her hands coming up to cover his as she pushed against him. She *knew* this game, revelled in it, and, heaven help them both, so did he.

With a ragged groan he wrapped his arms around her waist and her behind, carried her to the day-bed in the corner of the room, and tumbled her onto it.

Her clothes went, his did, and his need turned fierce.

He feasted on her lips, her skin, her breasts, and everywhere he touched she responded with a sigh, a shudder, a whimper. Tight, so tightly responsive, her eyes as black as her hair, hot colour riding high on her cheeks as he eased inside her, back and forth, each time filling her that little bit more.

She reared up beneath him, her hands clutching at his arms and her lips finding his for a kiss that seared clear through to his soul. He'd had lovers before, bedmates he'd enjoyed, but no one had *ever* played him like this. Not like this.

'More,' she whispered as he rolled onto his back, bringing her with him, still buried inside her.

'You'll get it.' He found her centre with his thumb, and she found a rhythm guaranteed to send him soaring, arching back, her breath coming in short sharp gasps. And then he was flying apart, touching the sky, taking her with him as he emptied himself into her and gave her what she asked for.

She laughed in the aftermath. Deliciously satisfied laughter that slid through Pete's body as he lay on his back, his hands still holding her in place while his muscles twitched and rippled in response to the demands he'd placed on them. So much for finesse. For taking his *time*. Taking the edge off his hunger for her.

The only thing he'd well and truly taken, he thought ruefully, was Serena. 'You okay?' he asked huskily. Not a question he normally had to ask. Usually, he made sure of it somewhere along the way. Usually, he didn't lose his *mind*.

'I swear I just went to heaven,' she said, and laughed some more. 'Am I dead?'

'You have a pulse.' He could feel it, intimately. 'You're not dead.' Judging by his returning hardness, neither was he. Yet.

'What's that?' she asked as he stirred inside her.

'A minor miracle.' Possibly an opportunity to show her he could be a civilised lover when he put his mind to it. Of course, first he had to *find* his mind. 'You did say you wanted more.'

Her lips curved as she trailed lazy fingers up his arms towards his shoulders. 'So I did.'

'I aim to please,' he told her, rolling her over onto her back before setting his lips to the corner of her mouth, the underside of her jaw, the curve of her neck, and then lower still, to a part of her he'd rushed over earlier.

'Oh, you do.' He closed his lips over her nipple and bit down gently, and she gasped and arched beneath him as her hands threaded though his hair, urgent and demanding. 'You really do.'

CHAPTER SIX

PETE BENNETT was both passionate and extremely thorough when he put his mind to it, decided Serena some half an hour later as she stood beneath a lukewarm shower. Pete had showered with her briefly, kissing her senseless beneath the spray, and, cursing her roundly as his body responded to hers again, had made himself scarce.

She watched him through the gap between the shower curtain and the cubicle as he dried off and pulled on his shorts and then his shirt. Such a tough, hard body. Such pleasure to be found from exploring it. He had another scar, in addition to the one on his shoulder. This one was nasty—a couple of centimetres wide running across his lower back. She couldn't be sure but it looked like a burn of some kind, maybe a rope burn, and she wondered what the hell had been on the other end of that rope to carve a gash that deep. He was a warrior, this man, never mind the façade. Beneath his reckless, charming ways lay the heart of a fighter.

Right this minute her warrior was a very sated man, she'd stake her life on it. His body had been to heaven

and back. She knew this because he'd taken her with him. His brain, on the other hand, didn't seem to have made the trip at all.

She stepped out of the shower and met his gaze in the mirror, hers questioning, his bleak.

'Light-hearted,' he said grimly.

'Yes.'

'And brief.'

'Yes.'

'Civilised.' His eyes were anything but.

'You forgot exclusive,' she told him.

'I didn't forget.' He turned around to scowl down at her, a thoroughly disgruntled dark angel, all the way from the spikes of his midnight black hair right down to his toes. 'This is a disaster,' he said as he pulled her closer. 'You're a disaster.' And with a kiss so unguardedly needy she trembled beneath the force of it, he turned on his heel and left the bathroom.

Pete sagged against the bathroom door the minute he closed it, willing himself not to go back in there, willing his feet to take him down the corridor and out of the cottage and to keep on walking, straight down the hill to the village. He needed to think. To regain the balance he'd lost in the arms of a siren.

One step. He dragged his extremely happy body away from the door and took it. And stopped abruptly as he looked up, straight at Nico—at Nico and Sam—who stood beside him.

'We're gonna cook the sea bass I caught this morning,' said Sam. 'Me and Nico. And we're inviting

Chloe and Serena and you to come and help us eat it for dinner.'

'Oh.' He struggled for words, for some sense of normality, a modicum of discretion, while Sam looked up at him hopefully and Nico eyed the bathroom door. 'How big is this fish?'

'Big,' said Sam with a grin. 'Where's Serena?'

Not a question he wanted to answer. 'She's been downloading the photos she took of you and Nico this morning onto her computer. I think she wants to use one of them for her postcard series. Go take a look. In the sitting room.'

Sam didn't need any more urging. Nico, on the other hand, stayed right where he was.

The bathroom door swung open the tiniest bit, an inch or so, nothing more, and Pete stepped in front of it, blocking Nico's view as he reached for the handle and pulled the door firmly closed.

Nico stared at him, studying his wet hair with a narrowed gaze. Pete stared back with not a lot to say. He tried putting himself in Nico's place. Tried to pretend he'd just caught some poor schmuck coming out of his sister's bathroom, with every indication of his sister still being in there. What would *he* do?

Castration seemed like a reasonable option.

Hopefully Nico was of a more civilised bent.

'You want to explain why that bathroom door suddenly seems to want to swing open by itself?' asked Nico silkily.

'Not really.' But for the sake of discretion he gave it a shot. 'Could be the wind.'

'Wind?' said Nico flatly.

'Uplift. Downdraft. Air. Wind.'

Nico didn't look convinced.

'O-or it could be that the door's set on a slant and swings open by itself.'

'It doesn't.'

'Pity.' He was running out of plausible excuses. 'Maybe it's possessed.'

Nico's lips twitched. 'Nice try.' But he wasn't buying it. 'Serena's a grown woman,' he said after a lengthy pause. 'She makes her own choices. I try and respect that.'

Castration didn't seem to have entered Nico's mind. This was a good thing.

And then Nico's gaze swung from Pete to the bathroom door and his face hardened. 'Hurt her and I'll hunt you down.'

Or maybe it had. 'No one's going to get hurt,' he said curtly. 'Serena knows what she's doing, and so do I.'

'Do you?' Nico rapped on the door with enough force to make it vibrate. 'Dinner's at seven. Chloe and Sam are eating with us,' he said loudly and stalked off.

No sooner had Nico disappeared than Serena stalked out, as fully dressed as a person could get in skimpy white shorts and a pink and lime bikini top. She glared at him, thoroughly miffed about something, possibly his parting shot about her being a disaster, but it was too late to take it back now. Besides, he didn't want to. 'What?' he said. What *now*?

'You call that discreet?'

'Well…yeah. It could have been worse.'

'How?' she demanded. 'Nico *knows* I was in there;

that you were in there with me. How on earth could it get any worse?'

'Hell, Serena,' he said, darkly amused by her indignation. 'Five minutes earlier and he'd have found us naked on the day-bed.'

Chloe arrived shortly after that and added her voice to the dinner invitation. 'It started with me offering to cook for you all at my place,' she told them ruefully as she set a big basket on the kitchen bench and turned to look back out the kitchen door to where Sam and Nico were cleaning the barbecue. 'I'm still not sure how the invitation got turned around to having it here. I hope you don't mind. I brought the fixings for a salad with me and some bread and wine. Nico says he's cooking the fish.'

'I love it when he says that,' said Serena.

'So you don't mind?' Chloe turned towards her and Pete, her expression faintly apologetic. 'You weren't planning to go out to dinner? Just the two of you?'

'Well…we could?' said Pete. 'I hadn't thought much about dinner at all. Yet.' He caught her gaze, a question in his, and that small act of courtesy and uncertainty after all that had gone before was Serena's undoing.

'If we stay here I can guarantee us a glass of wine or beer with dinner,' she said lightly, opening the fridge and raiding it for both items and setting them on the counter. She had no idea how much their disastrously wonderful lovemaking had changed things. Absolutely no idea what he wanted from her. All she knew was that he was welcome at her table and that she didn't want him to leave. 'Matter of fact I can guarantee them now.'

'There is that,' he said, with the whisper of a smile.

'So you'll stay for dinner?' said Chloe hopefully. 'The more the merrier, I say.' She didn't want to dine alone with Sam and Nico was what she *meant*. 'There'll be plenty of food.'

There was that word again, thought Serena wryly. Plenty. She looked at Pete and that was exactly what she saw. 'Here.' She passed him the beer, got another bottle from the fridge and a lemonade for Sam and handed those to him as well. 'Go help Nico and Sam man the barbecue while Chloe and I get busy in the kitchen.'

'Does this feel light-hearted to you?' he muttered, shooting her an enigmatic glance as she held the kitchen screen door open to let him through. 'It doesn't feel light hearted to me. Feels kind of family-oriented.'

'I know.' She smiled wryly. 'But stay anyway.'

Having Pete stay on for dinner was a bigger mistake than she'd thought it would be, decided Serena an hour later as she sat at the garden table and watched him bond with Sam and Nico over slow-barbecued potatoes and soon-to-be-barbecued sea bass. She didn't want to notice the way Sam looked up to him, or how much Nico seemed to enjoy his company, never mind Nico's earlier words of warning outside the bathroom door. Pete Bennett charmed without thinking, without understanding what it would do to a woman fresh from his lovemaking to watch him interact so easily with the people she loved.

'If I were a betting woman—which I'm not,' said Chloe, coming up beside her and handing her one of the two glasses of champagne she held in her hands, and sipping delicately on the other, 'I'd say the universe you've been contemplating of late was standing right there by the barbecue. And what a universe it is,' she murmured with a wicked smile, and Serena felt her own lips curve in reluctant agreement.

'It's only a temporary universe,' she told Chloe. 'He'll be leaving soon. *I'll* be leaving soon.'

'Haven't we just had this conversation?' said Chloe dryly.

'No, that was a different conversation. You and Nico have a shot at something beautiful. Pete and I…well…he's going in one direction and I'm going in another. I don't *want* to change direction to accommodate him.'

'Perhaps he'll change direction to accommodate you.'

The thought slid through her, bright and beckoning, demanding closer examination.

'He's very good with Sam,' said Chloe. 'He cares for people.'

She'd noticed. And all of a sudden she was standing there wondering just what kind of father he would make, what kind of husband. And what it would take to capture his heart.

No.

Some other woman could glory in his passionate lovemaking and delight in the compassion beneath his strength. Not her.

Some other woman could heal a heart too heavy and too wounded to carry any more loss. *Not* her. She had dreams of her own to chase. Dreams that didn't involve him.

Serena tore her gaze away from Pete to stare out at the ocean with a growing sense of panic.

If only she could remember what they were.

It was almost ten p.m. when Chloe deemed it time for her and Sam to head back to the village. Dinner had been served and savoured and Sam was fading fast in the wake of his early morning. Pete stood as well, offering to walk back to the hotel with them, and the happy family picture the three of them made set Serena's eyes to narrowing. Never mind that it wasn't real, Serena didn't like it. Neither did Nico.

'Aren't you going to walk down with them?' she muttered to her cousin.

'Aren't you?' he countered darkly.

'No.'

Nico scowled. 'I'll join you,' he said to them abruptly.

Pete nodded, as if he'd expected no less, and started clearing plates and empty glasses from the table, carrying them into the kitchen while Nico helped Chloe and Sam gather their belongings ready for departure. Better, much better.

'What time are you heading out in the morning?' she asked him lightly as he set the dishes on the sink. No pressure. No clinging. Much.

'Around ten. My clients want to go to Santorini.'

Santorini. Plenty of night-life in Santorini. 'Staying overnight there, are you?'

'Yeah.' He leaned forward and kissed her cheek.

'What was that?'

'Discreet.'

Oh. She thought of him not being around tomorrow, or the day after that. Thought of the pleasure to be found in his kisses and decided to scrap discretion and go with need instead. She ached for his touch, for what it could bring, and she dumped her own armful of dishes into the sink, stepped in close and touched her lips to his, teasing at first, and then ravenously hungry as she dragged them deeper and deeper into uncharted waters.

'I'll call you,' he said raggedly when at last the kiss ended. 'I'll be back. Soon. As soon as I can.'

'I'll be here,' she said and felt her heart tremble. 'For the next couple of weeks.'

Pete called her mid-afternoon the following day.

'Where are you?' she wanted to know.

'Sitting in a café in Santorini, reading the paper.'

Lucky him. She was sitting beneath the beach umbrella beside the Vespa shed.

'How do you feel about working for a fashion photography house in New York?' he asked her.

'Unenthusiastic.' She leaned back in her chair. 'Although it does satisfy the requirement of being some distance from my family.'

'Just checking,' he said. 'Wedding photographer in Vegas?'

'Only if I'd be working for Elvis.'

'It's possible.' She could feel the smile in his voice, closed her eyes and let it warm her through. 'Okay, here's something you might be more interested in. It's a photography competition and it's global. They want you to capture and celebrate the essence of humanity.'

'I'm listening.'

'I'm glad. I'll bring you the details.'

'When?'

'Soon.'

Serena sighed. She knew what soon meant. It meant he had no idea when he'd be back. 'Enjoy Santorini. It's a pretty place.'

'You're prettier,' he said, and disconnected.

He phoned her again the following day. This time she was ready for him.

'What are you doing?' Pete asked her.

'The crossword in *The Sydney Morning Herald*.' She was sitting in her usual place beneath the beach umbrella by the old Vespa shed, but time was passing more quickly this morning. 'A British rock god needs a helicopter pilot to keep on retainer.'

'Just shoot me now,' he said.

'Just checking. There's also a need for a medivac helicopter pilot along the Northern Australian seaboard.'

Silence.

'I'm sensing some reluctant interest in that one,' she said with a grin. 'I'll keep the paper for you. Meanwhile I have a job interview in Athens tomorrow with a big daily newspaper. They're after a photojournalist who can cover politics one day and human-interest stories the next. It sounds promising.'

'How are you getting there?' he asked her.

'I thought I'd take the ferry.'

'I can get you there faster than a ferry,' he muttered. He could get her there faster than anybody on the planet, and she was pretty sure he knew it. 'Are you free tomorrow? I could hire your charter services.'

'You can have them for free. When's your interview?'

'Four in the afternoon.'

'I'll come for you at midday. We can go out for a meal afterwards. Spend the night in Athens. If you've a mind to.'

'I'd love to.' She already had a teenager from the village organised to take charge of the Vespas for a day. Why not for two days? She had good reason, and heaven help her she had a fierce need to spend some time alone with Pete without having to be discreet about it. 'I've missed you, flyboy.'

'I want you in my arms again,' he told her, with a rasp to his voice that set her skin to tingling. 'Preferably sitting on my lap.'

He wasn't the only one. 'Am I naked?'

'Very.'

'Are *you* naked?'

'I'm at the airport in Athens. If I was I'd be arrested.'

'So…I'll see you tomorrow, then?'

'I'll come for you,' he said.

She was counting on it.

CHAPTER SEVEN

THERE was a world of difference between life on a sleepy Greek island and the vibrant energy that came with being in the middle of a major city. People moved faster, talked louder, dressed smarter and for the most part looked a whole lot tenser. Six months ago Serena would have thrived on the bustle and the crowds. Now she found it slightly unnerving.

Or maybe it was just the thought of the up-coming job interview that unnerved her.

She and Pete were standing outside the newsgroup building. It was almost time to head inside. She'd gathered her hair up into an elegant chignon and had donned a charcoal-grey business suit for the occasion. She looked good. If her portfolio of work was any sharper it'd grow fangs and bite someone. The only thing missing was her enthusiasm for walking through those double glass doors.

'Time to go, Rena,' he said as she looked at the doors for the tenth time in half as many minutes.

'How do I look?' she asked him.

'Smart. Sophisticated. Like you belong here.'

'Really?' He was wearing cargo trousers, a collared shirt and a smile that scattered her wits. No charcoal-coloured business suit for him and he still managed to look more at home on these streets than she did. How did he do that? She fiddled nervously with the collar on her shirt, scrunching it up; Pete smoothed it out.

'Where's your confidence?' he said, tilting her chin up with his forefinger so that her gaze met his.

'Gone.'

'Happens that way sometimes.' He pressed his lips to her cheek, a man who knew not to mess with lipstick at a time like this. 'Time to remember who you are. What you are. And what you want.'

Oh, boy. It'd help if she *knew*. 'I could use a reminder.'

'You're talented, educated, smart, savvy, and determined.'

'You're right,' she said straightening. 'I am.'

'You want this job?'

'I do.'

He put his hands to her shoulders and turned her in the direction of the door. 'Go get it.'

Pete watched the traffic go by while he waited for Serena's interview to finish, wondering at her last-minute hesitation. He knew her best when she wore gypsy skirts and sleeveless cotton shirts, but it came as no surprise to him that she could look perfectly at home in a business suit. If she wanted this kind of life all she had to do was reach out and take it. He was that certain of her talent and her ability to succeed.

She didn't belong on the island; anyone with eyes could see that. Whether she belonged *here* was up to her.

It was a quarter to five before she reappeared. He figured it for a good sign. 'How'd it go?' he asked her when she stood in front of him.

'It was a panel interview,' she told him, chewing on her lower lip. 'There were five of them. It was hard to tell what they thought—either collectively or individually.' She lifted her chin a fraction. 'They said I'd hear from them in a few days. *I* thought it went well.'

'Hold that thought.' He slung his arm around her shoulders, she wrapped her arm around his waist and together they started walking. 'Where to now?' he asked her. 'Dinner? A drink? A show?'

'Yes,' she said with a vigorous nod for good measure. 'All of them.'

'Any particular order?'

'Surprise me.'

He did surprise her. He took her to the art gallery Medusa where a modern photographic exhibition was showing, and fed her creativity. After that he took her to dinner at a restaurant that boasted candlelit corners, Spanish cuisine, and a Lebanese entertainer with a repertoire ranging from 'Zorba the Greek' to 'Dancing Queen'. The meal fed her stomach, the entertainment fed her sense of humour. The place was a mish-mashing clash of cultures with a boisterous crowd, a little bit of whimsy, and plenty of romance thrown in for free and it matched her mood perfectly. *He* matched her mood perfectly, played to it, and at the end of the evening when the music slowed he took her into his arms and the night turned to magic.

'What next?' he murmured when the music drew to a close.

'You and me,' she said without hesitation. 'Alone.' Always it came back to this.

The colours from the streetlights played over his face, such a beautiful face, as he hailed them a taxi. He didn't touch her on the way back to the hotel, not until they reached the lift and then it was only to put his palm to the small of her back as they stepped inside. His hand dropped away after that. He looked like a man with a lot on his mind, not all of it welcome.

'Penny for them,' she said.

His smile belonged to a rogue but his eyes were somewhat more sombre. 'I was wondering what you'd do if you landed this job. Where you'd live… Who'd take charge of the Vespas…'

'I'd probably stay with my aunt and uncle—Nico's parents—for a while until I found a place of my own.'

'And the Vespas?'

'Currently have my second cousin Marina's name on them. It's her turn to come and contemplate the universe for a while.'

'You didn't mind it that much,' he said dryly.

'You're right,' she admitted. 'I didn't. I got to take some beautiful pictures and live in a beautiful part of the world. But I wouldn't want to do it on a permanent basis. It wouldn't satisfy me. It's not enough.'

'And the job you went for today will be enough?' he asked her as they reached the hotel room.

'Maybe,' she muttered as he ushered her inside. She didn't know. 'If I get it I guess I'll find out. But it's a step in the right direction, that's the main thing. I've already spent too much time doing things I never really wanted to do, mainly to keep my family happy.' She shrugged out of her jacket and slipped off her shoes with a sigh of relief. 'I got my photography and language qualifications by fitting them in around the work I've done in the family businesses. Had I wanted to be a restaurateur like my brother, or had a vision for growing and marketing the seafood arm of the business like my sister, everything would have worked out just fine, but unfortunately I don't want to do either of those things. I want to tell stories. Take photos that tell stories. *Use* those qualifications it took me so long to get.' Pete said nothing, just watched and listened. 'You probably think I'm selfish,' she said, turning away from him so she wouldn't see the confirmation in his eyes. She'd heard that particular opinion voiced often enough times over the years that she'd learned to anticipate it, brace for it. 'That I should appreciate all the opportunities my family have given me and take one of them.'

'If you're waiting for me to tell you to sacrifice your own needs for those of your family you'll be waiting a long time, Serena,' he said, punctuating his words with a tiny tilt of his lips. 'I lit out of home as soon as the Navy would have me, chasing the sky and a childhood dream. I left behind a grieving father, an older brother, two younger brothers, and a sister—all of whom needed me—because I had to go my own way. I know what it is to sacrifice family for freedom. I've done it.' His lips twisted. 'The worst part is when they tell you to go and that they'll be there when you need them and that they're proud of you for going after what you want.'

'I'd have been proud of you too,' she said quietly. 'If you'd been mine.' His words had comforted her, settled her conscience. He knew what it was to chase a dream. He understood.

'Tell your family what you've just told me,' he said. 'Hell, just show them your photos. If that doesn't convince them you're wasted on the fishing business, nothing will.'

'They've seen them. To them photography is just a hobby, something to do on the side. Photojournalism is marginally more acceptable.'

His eyes narrowed. 'So which one would *you* prefer to spend your time doing? Straight photography or photojournalism?'

Now there was a question. One she'd spent a great deal of time trying to answer. 'For the sheer joy of it? Probably the photography.'

'In that case why the *hell* did you just go for a photojournalist job?'

His voice was curt, his expression formidable. Maybe he didn't understand quite as much as she thought. 'It gets me good subject material for my camera. It's a time-honoured road for photographers to take. The job might not be perfect, but moments of it will be, and those are the ones I'll savour. 'She sent him a wry smile. 'Surely you of all people can understand that.'

He laughed abruptly; it seemed he could.

'But enough about work,' she said lightly. Here they were in a room with a blissfully large bed in it and an entire night at their disposal. Her thoughts turned wicked as she started pulling pins from her hair, the ones that had kept her businesslike chignon in place. 'I'd like a shower,' she said, shaking her hair free and dropping the pins on the bedside table before padding towards the minibar, her stockinged feet sinking into the deliciously plush carpet. 'A glass of wine…' She opened the fridge, selected a bottle and tossed it on the bed. 'Some chocolate…' She perused the selection on top of the counter, chose the Swiss variety, and tossed that on the bed too. 'I know it sounds trite but I'd like to slip into something a little more comfortable.' She had a white silk cami and matching panties in her luggage. She found them, threw them onto the bed as well. 'And then I'd like you.' She looked meaningfully at the pile on the bed and then back at Pete. Pete's lips twitched. 'Feel free to arrange yourself any way you like.'

'I'd like to oblige,' he said. 'Really. And I'm sure we can come to some sort of mutually agreeable arrangement at some point in time.' He was peeling off his shirt as he spoke, heading towards her, grabbing her by the hand. 'But *my* fantasy started the minute you mentioned the shower.'

He made her laugh as he turned on the shower taps and pulled them both under the spray, and her still fully dressed. Made her gasp as he peeled her out of her clothes and set about devouring her body.

Later, much later, he wrapped her in a towel, carried her to the bed and fed her wine and chocolate as she relived the high points of her interview for him, and the low. And then the wine and chocolate went on the counter and the towel went on the floor and he reached for her again.

This time, the sheer perfection and intensity of his lovemaking nearly made her cry.

Pete flew her home the following morning, his body utterly exhausted and his mind fogged with the pleasure only Serena's touch could bring. He'd had lovers before. Generous, accomplished lovers, but not one of them had ever brought to lovemaking what Serena gave to him.

A sensuality that held him breathless. A generosity that left him reeling.

And a hunger for more that he didn't know how to deal with.

She had to get back to Sathi. He had to get her there and then go take care of Tomas's business. That was his agenda for today. He couldn't think any further than that. He didn't want to think further than that. Because then he'd start thinking about what he'd begun to want from this woman and it had for ever written all over it.

And he sure as hell didn't want to think about *that*.

So he took her home and he played the game she'd asked of him and grinned at the scene that greeted him when they touched down in Sathi.

There was no shark, no ten-inch boning knives, no father and uncle with narrow-eyed glares and faces carved from rock. But Theo was sitting on the bench across from the helipad sharpening a box full of frighteningly large fish hooks and the majestically built Marianne Papadopoulos was there as well, pounding octopus on a flat weathered rock with a glint to her eye and a strength to her wrist that put him in mind of a cat o nine tails and some poor unsuspecting sod's back.

It was a warning, beautifully executed, almost effective. Serena slid him a long-suffering glance. Pete grinned at her.

'This is the part where you *leave*,' she told him dryly.

'I knew that,' he said.

'And never come back.'

'Now that's unlikely.' He gave Theo a nod, Marianne Papadopoulos a smile he reserved for the hardest of hearts and laughed when she narrowed her eyes and stopped pounding in favour of grinding that octopus hard against the rock with a swift, twisting motion. 'I'll be back,' he said and lightly bussed her lips. 'Count on it.'

CHAPTER EIGHT

WHEN it came to women and the wooing of them, Pete Bennett could justify just about any hare-brained scheme. Everything from a daily bombardment of flowers to remote location helicopter joyrides with a picnic basket and blanket packed for good measure. From tandem parachute jumps to Symphony Orchestra concerts by way of a spot of deep-sea marlin fishing in between. But he'd never, ever, done anything as stupid as jumping in a helicopter when he should have been working and setting off for a sleepy little Greek island that no one else seemed to want to go to on the off chance that once he got there the ache around his heart might ease.

He *should* have been checking into an Athens hotel, grabbing a bite to eat, and bedding down early in readiness for the five a.m. start his clients had requested the following day. He had a schedule to stick to, passengers to collect. He should have *phoned* Serena when he'd got the urge to talk to her. That was what a sane man would have done.

Instead he was flying the little Jet Ranger fast and low

en route to Sathi, his mind firmly fixed on getting to his destination before the sun disappeared over the horizon.

After that…well…after that he didn't much care what he did so long as Serena was a part of it.

Pete touched down just on dusk, secured the rotors, and locked the little helicopter down for the night before finally heading for Chloe's hotel. Discretion. He knew the need for it, tried to think of a way to act with it and still make contact with Serena. He pulled his phone out of his pocket and dialled. 'Where are you?' he said when she answered the phone.

'Halfway down the goat track,' she said somewhat breathlessly. 'And if that wasn't you in that damned helicopter I'm going to strangle you.'

Always nice to feel appreciated. Pete grinned. 'Have dinner with me.'

'Where?'

'Anywhere. I'm heading for Chloe's.'

'I'm two steps in front of you. Is it too late to be coy about dinner and tell you I'll check my calendar and get back to you?'

'How fast are you coming down that hill?'

'Fast.'

'It's too late. Besides, coy doesn't suit you. Neither does discreet. Feel free to jump me in the foyer.'

'Keep dreaming,' she said. 'I can be *very* discreet when I need to be. Get a room. Order something from room service. And wait.'

'If there's a God this fantasy will include you, a short black skirt, a frilly white apron, and not a lot else.'

'God is not a minimalist,' she told him blithely. 'God is bountiful.'

'Amen,' he muttered, and finished the call before he fell over his feet in his haste.

'No,' Chloe told Serena sternly. 'You can *not* be a room-service maid. Nico would kill you. Then he'd kill me for letting you.'

'Who's going to tell him?' countered Serena, not begging, not yet. 'Not me.'

'This is Sathi, Serena. Everyone will tell him because five minutes after I put you behind the room-service trolley everyone will know. Wait. Meet the man in public, where everyone can see what you're doing. And what you're not.'

'But I *told* him to call for room service.'

'And I'll tell him he can't have any. Anticipation is good for a man.'

'That's all well and good, Chloe, but it's killing *me*.'

'You need a distraction.'

'He *is* the distraction,' she said earnestly.

'Then you need another distraction. Here, read the paper. I circled a job in there for you.'

'What is it with people thrusting newspapers with job applications in them at me?' she grumbled, reluctantly taking the paper Chloe held out to her.

'Gee,' said Chloe. 'Could it have something to do with your burning ambition to leave this place and make your mark on the world?'

There was that.

'You can read it in my office,' said Chloe.

'Why can't I read it here at the reception desk?' While waiting for Superman to show up.

'Office,' said Chloe. 'I mean it. Think of your reputation. Everyone else will be. And if that doesn't stop you think of your family.'

'I'm going,' she muttered darkly. 'But I want you to know you ruined a perfectly good fantasy. My body hates you.'

'There's baklava in the office. Marianne Papadopoulos brings it in as payment for letting her use one of the tables in the taverna for her bridge game.'

'My body forgives you.'

'Your body is fickle.'

'No, it's just a sucker for perfection in all its many and varied forms.'

'Office,' said Chloe. 'And stay there 'til Pilot Pete has gone to his room.'

'I'd like a room,' Pete said to Chloe, his duffel at his feet and his anticipation running rampant.

'And it's nice to see you again too,' she said dryly, leaning against the counter and all but ignoring the credit card he held out to her. Finally, she took it and proceeded to open the bookings ledger with not nearly enough haste for his liking. 'Looking for someone?' she added as he scanned the foyer for a wanton goddess wielding a room-service cart.

'If I were being indiscreet I'd say Serena, but I'm not so I can't. And it's nice to see you too, Chloe. How's Sam?'

'Waiting impatiently for the weekend, so he can go out fishing with Nico again. What kind of room?'

'Any room.' He paused to reconsider. 'Something out of the way. Possibly soundproof, with a domed-glass roof and a view of the hinder stars.'

'Uh-huh.'

A slight sound came from the direction of Chloe's office, just behind the reception desk. The door was almost shut. Almost but not quite. 'Did you just whimper?'

'Excuse me?'

'Never mind.'

'You can have room seventeen, the same room you were in last time,' she said. 'Or I can offer you a smaller room, discreetly placed at the back of the hotel.'

'You *have* seen Serena.'

'Uh-huh.'

'So how do I order room service?'

'You don't. Nico heard you fly in, along with half the island's population. Theo's here, Marianne Papadopoulos is here. The room service you require is not available right now. Have a drink or a meal in the taverna instead. Nico might join you there. Then perhaps Serena and I later on.'

'So...no room service?' he said.

'None whatsoever.'

'No glass ceiling and view of the stars?'

'Lie on your side and look out the window.'

'Chloe, Chloe, Chloe,' he chided with a grin. 'Where's the romance in your soul?'

'Buried beneath the weight of my responsibilities, which for some reason have grown to include both you and Serena. You don't know this place or the people here. Even if you care nothing for your own reputation you need to think of Serena's and that of her family. Trust me on this.'

'I do trust you, Chloe. Which is why I'll take your advice,' he said with a sigh as he kissed his French-maid fantasies goodbye. 'Any more advice?'

'Yeah, it's Theo and Marianne's bridge night in there at table two and they're a player short. Resist. And Peter…'

He waited.

'I realise seduction comes as naturally to you as breathing, but try and travel a little slower than the speed of light this evening. Seduction's frowned upon around these parts. Try something else.'

'Like what?'

'You could always try courtship.'

Courtship. Right. 'As in bring a goat along for Serena's grandfather?'

'She's Greek, Peter, not a Bedouin.'

'So…no goat?'

'Just respect her.'

'You think I don't?'

'I think women come easily to you and always have. I think you don't know the difference between courtship and seduction.' She handed him the key. Not room seventeen. 'And I think it's time you learned.'

Pete made it to the out-of-the-way room at the back of the hotel, set his bag by the bed, took a fast shower and changed into fresh trousers and a collared white shirt. He could use a haircut, he decided after checking his appearance in the mirror. His hair was getting more and more like Tris's mop, less and less like Luke's regulation crew cut, but then, he didn't need a crew cut these days anyway. He wasn't Navy any more.

He didn't know what he was.

Hungry, he was that, and Chloe had suggested he head for the hotel taverna. Hopefully he'd find Nico there already. There were worse chaperons. Then again, Nico might not be there at all. He might end up sitting there alone, which wouldn't bode well for him when it came to resisting bridge invitations. He needed something to do while he waited, figured it might as well be the mail and paperwork he was supposed to have waded through a week ago.

Make that two weeks ago, he decided, eyeing the bulging black folder in his carryall with trepidation. He could run the flying component of Tomas's business with his eyes closed. The paperwork and scheduling side, however, was a nightmare.

Tomas was out of hospital and starting to get up and around. Maybe if Pete got the paperwork up to date Tomas could take the running of that part of the business *back*. Pete picked up the folder and headed for the door, no further incentive required. He'd do it while he waited.

Except that Nico was already at the taverna when he got there, looking tired and not altogether sociable. Still, he nodded when he saw him and Pete figured it for an invitation of sorts.

'So how'd they get you down here midway through a working week?' he said by way of greeting.

'Chloe rang and said she needed me,' said Nico

offering up a wry grin. 'A statement guaranteed to get me down here any time of night, or day, for that matter. Then she mentioned you, Serena, room service, Theo, and Marianne Papadopoulos in her next breath and that was the end of *that* fantasy.'

'I know the feeling,' said Pete with heartfelt sincerity. 'What do you know about courtship?'

'Do you see Chloe standing here, breathless to be in my company?'

'No.'

'Exactly,' said Nico darkly. 'I've been here almost six months and I still can't get her to notice me. I know *nothing* about courtship.'

'But I do see her and Sam over in the doorway waving at you.'

Nico turned sharply, his face splitting into a grin, and then he was heading towards them. Maybe he knew more about courting than he thought. The middle-aged barman behind the counter removed Nico's empty beer glass. 'I'll have one of those,' Pete told the barman.

'No beer for you,' said the barman. 'You can have coffee.'

'In that case, I'll have it at a table.' He took himself and his paperwork towards a corner table, only to be stopped by the majestically built Mrs Papadopoulos greeting him and wanting to know how Tomas was. 'He's out of hospital and up walking around,' said Pete. 'The cast comes off in another few weeks.'

'So you will leave us, once he mends, eh?' she countered.

'That's the plan.'

'Plans change,' said the lady. 'Isn't that right, Theo?'

Theo scowled.

'Tell me, Peter,' she continued, thoroughly undaunted by Theo's surly demeanour. 'Do you play bridge?'

'Never did get the hang of it, Mrs Papadopoulos. Besides, I have some paperwork to see to.'

'And friends to greet,' she said, eyeing the doorway behind him. 'The taverna's a busy place, this evening.'

He turned, following her gaze, and there stood Serena, looking exceedingly demure in an ankle length yellow sundress that, if he had to hazard a guess, he'd say belonged to Chloe. And then she smiled and he wouldn't have been able to describe what she was wearing. 'Excuse me.'

He made it to the door without falling over his feet, made it through small talk with Chloe and saying hello to Sam, who had homework and then bed to look forward to rather than socialising in the taverna, according to Chloe.

'I could stay here for a while,' said Sam. 'With Nico and Pete and Serena. I'm not tired.'

'Not on a school night,' said Chloe and Sam's frown turned mutinous.

'I'll do my homework in the morning.'

'You've had all afternoon to do it. You'll do it tonight.'

'Homework being part of the renegotiated deal involving Sam fishing with Nico on Saturday *and* Sunday mornings,' murmured Serena.

'Ah.'

'Do what your aunt says,' said Nico. 'She gives you

more freedom than I ever had as a boy, and receives more than her share of criticism because of it. Cut her a break, Sam, and honour your bargain.'

Sam's face grew even more thunderous, but he turned on his heel and stalked through the hotel without another word. Nico watched him go with a frown. 'A boy needs limits,' he said finally.

'When I want your help, Nicholas Comino,' said Chloe icily, 'I'll ask for it!' And then she too was gone and silence reigned supreme.

'I'm pretty sure she'll be back,' said Pete finally.

Serena nodded. 'Me too.'

Nico glared at them both. 'And if she doesn't come back?'

'Beer?' said Pete.

'Bridge?' said Serena, looking towards Theo and Mrs Papadopoulos.

'I like his suggestion better,' said Nico. '*You* play bridge.'

Serena shook her head emphatically. 'I like his suggestion better too. I was just giving you options.'

'The man doesn't need options, Serena. He needs hope,' said Pete. He thought of seduction and of courtship and wondered where a compliment might fit in the grand scheme of things. 'And may I say you're looking divine this evening, as usual. Care to join me and my melancholy friend here for a drink?'

'You can have ten minutes,' she told him with a toss of her head. 'Then I'm off to check on Chloe. She's a little sensitive right now to the influence Nico has over Sam.'

'And you couldn't have mentioned this earlier?' demanded Nico, shooting her a dark glare.

Serena shot him a halfway apologetic glance. 'I thought you knew.'

'I'm curious,' said Pete, steering them both towards a table. 'Does Nico supporting Chloe's authority over Sam count as courtship or seduction?'

'Pardon?' said Serena.

'I'm saved,' he told Nico. 'She doesn't know either.'

'Huh?' said Nico.

'Never mind. Coffee?' he asked Serena. 'Have you eaten?'

'No, and no. But I'd rather have wine with my meal than coffee.'

'Good luck with that,' he murmured, and turned to browse the blackboard menu. 'What's good here?'

'The fish,' said Nico dryly. 'I caught it this morning. And *I'll* order the wine.'

They got their wine but held off on ordering meals in favour of waiting to see if Chloe returned.

'Bring any passengers in?' asked Nico.

'They're still in Athens. I'll go back for them in the morning. They're booked to go to Kos.' Pete relaxed back into his chair, more content than he'd been at any point during the last two days. 'Was my coming here tonight on the off chance of meeting up with Serena an act of courtship or seduction, do you think?'

Nico shook his head. 'Hell, I've got it pegged as an act of desperation.'

'I think it was sweet,' said Serena, favouring him with a smile. 'What's in the folder?'

'Mail and scheduling paperwork in case I ended up sitting here by myself. Chloe warned me about the bridge party. I figured I might need a prop.'

'Good move.' Serena flicked open the folder and began to browse. 'Aerial cattle mustering in the Northern Territory? Really?'

He'd forgotten about the job ads he'd shoved in there. 'It could be fun,' he said.

'Yeah, for about five minutes.'

'It's seasonal, Serena. Read on. Five minutes is as long as it takes.'

'I was thinking of it as a more permanent position.'

'No.'

'Oh.' She flicked over to the next page. Pete sighed. This one involved transporting men and supplies to and from oilrigs off the Western Australian coastline and this one *was* permanent. Doubtless he'd hear her opinion on it too.

'It's not exactly family-oriented, is it?' she said after a read through.

'It doesn't need to be,' he countered. 'Does it?'

'I'm just saying that it's something you might want to think about if you're looking at a long term position, that's all.'

'Interesting advice,' he said mildly. 'Coming from you.'

Nico snorted, Serena ignored them both, turning that paper over to stare down at the next one. A fax this time, marked urgent, and not strictly a job advertisement. 'What's this?'

'Private.'

She looked up, her startled gaze clashing with his.

'Sorry.' She shut the folder and pushed it back towards him. Yours, her actions said, but there was a question in her eyes and on her lips. Knowing Serena, it wouldn't be long before she voiced it.

'They want you back, don't they? They've asked you to go back and fly rescue helicopters for them again.'

He didn't reply. Didn't think he needed to. It was Nico who broke the silence. 'Your ten minutes is up, Serena. It's time to go find Chloe. Please,' he added.

'For you,' she told her cousin as she scraped back her chair and stood to leave. 'Because I love you and I know she'll come round. You'll see. And as for you…' Pete found himself on the receiving end of an apologetic smile. 'I'm sorry I pried. Even sorrier about the lack of room service. But I *am* glad you're here.'

Serena found Sam and Chloe in Chloe's tiny two-bedroom apartment nestled at the back of the hotel grounds. Sam looked up from his seat at the kitchen table but there was no smile for her as she greeted him. Instead he nodded curtly and turned his attention back to the schoolbooks surrounding him. Chloe stood at the kitchen bench chopping salad ingredients into a bowl. A steaming dish of moussaka sat cooling on the stove. Sam still looked mutinous. Chloe still looked upset. The silence pervading the room could have been heard over a full scale military tattoo it was that loud. 'So… you're eating over here?' she said lightly.

'Yes.'

'How about joining us for coffee a little later, then?'

'I can't, Serena.'

'You're angry with Nico.'

'I'm angry with everyone, including myself,' said Chloe tightly.

Wholesale anger. Not good. 'You need company. Anger loves company.'

'You mean misery.'

'Exactly. So we'll all come and eat over here with you and Sam, then, shall we?'

Chloe picked up a knife and began dicing carrots, dumping them into an already overflowing salad bowl. Clearly Chloe hadn't been paying a whole lot of attention to the amount of salad she actually needed when she'd been cutting it up. Serena looked from the salad to the oversized casserole dish full of fragrant moussaka. 'How many people were you planning on feeding tonight?'

Sam looked up briefly and caught her eye, a smile tugging at his lips before he ducked his head and went back to his homework.

'C'mon, Chloe,' she said quietly. 'Nico's beside himself. He thinks he's hurt you. Both of you.'

Chloe remained silent, so did Sam.

'He was only trying to help.'

More silence.

'You think walking a line between what you want and what Sam wants is easy? It damn near rips my cousin in two sometimes, Chloe. He doesn't deserve your anger.' Sam slid her another furtive glance from his spot at the table. 'And he certainly doesn't deserve yours,' she told him bluntly. 'Finished your homework yet?'

Sam nodded warily. 'Just now.'

'Perfect,' she said, turning back to Chloe. 'Sam's ready to eat. We're all ready to eat. And here you are with enough food to feed a dozen people. Invite us over. It'll make everyone feel better.'

'What do you think, Sam?' said Chloe faintly. 'Shall we invite them over here for dinner?'

Sam shrugged. 'It's your house. Your food.'

'Yours too,' said Chloe.

Sam looked away, all shut down.

Chloe looked down at the bench, but not before Serena caught the sheen of tears in her eyes. She reached up and tucked a strand of Chloe's straight dark hair back behind her ear with gentle fingers. Chloe looked up and shot her a miserable smile. 'Sorry,' she whispered.

'Don't be. Just send Sam to go get Nico and Pete. I'll stay here and help you set the table. Trust me. It'll be fun. It'll work.' She reached over to the little radio by the kitchen sink and switched it on. 'We'll make it work.'

Pete wasn't averse to having dinner at Chloe's place rather than the taverna. Judging by the swiftness with which Nico pushed back his chair and stood to leave, neither was he. 'What about the gossip?' Pete asked Nico, surreptitiously eyeing the formidably gossipy Marianne Papadopoulos and co. Gossip being the reason they'd all been meeting at the taverna in full view of everyone in the first place. 'Will having us to dinner be a problem for Chloe?'

'Do I look like I *care*?' said Nico.

Good point.

They had to pass the bridge party table on the way out. Pete nodded to them. Nico went one better. Nico stopped.

'I need some flowers,' he said to Marianne Papadopoulos.

She pursed her lips, her old eyes shrewd. 'Happens I have a garden full of them. I'm open to trading suggestions.'

'Two kilos of fish from tomorrow's catch,' said Nico, ignoring the amused glances of the other card players at the table. 'For a fistful of whatever I like from your garden.'

A glimmer of a smile played about those thin wrinkled lips. 'My scented pink roses are in flower,' she said with the air of someone bestowing something special. 'They're not just any old flower. You want some of those, you'll need to trade up.'

Nico eyed her narrowly. 'The *best* of tomorrow's catch for the best in your garden.'

Marianne's smile bloomed. 'Agreed.'

'I need them now,' he said.

'You can have them now. Mind you use the secateurs hanging on the tool shed door to cut them. I'll have no ragged stems in my garden.'

'Anyone care to concentrate on the *cards*?' asked Theo, his voice long-suffering.

'Ho! Listen to you!' said Marianne Papadopoulos. 'Was a time you asked for flowers from my garden in just the same way, old goat!'

'I gave them back to you, didn't I?'

Nico snorted. Theo glared. Pete edged away from the table, Sam was right behind him. The boy had a good eye for a fast brewing storm. Best not to get caught in the eye of it.

'I'll meet you up at Chloe's,' said Nico when they reached the hotel grounds. 'You two go on ahead.' He strode off down the laneway in the direction of the village. Sam looked after him, his expression wistful.

The boy had delivered Chloe's invitation with a wariness Pete had found painful to watch, and he wasn't nearly as invested in the kid as Nico. Nico had probably found it excruciating.

'Reckon I can find my own way to Chloe's apartment if you'd rather go with Nico,' he told the boy, offhand.

'He wouldn't want me around,' mumbled Sam.

Pete shrugged. 'I say he would. Matter of fact I think it'd mean a lot to him if you helped him pick those flowers for Chloe.'

Sam slanted him a gaze. 'You don't know that.'

'You're right, I don't. But that's what I think.'

Sam stared at him, his face a study of indecision as hope warred with fear. And then the boy was racing after Nico, falling into step beside him and shoving his hands in his pockets for good measure. Not a word passed between them but Nico slowed to accommodate the boy and the shadow of a smile flitted across the kid's face.

'Guess I was right,' he murmured, and, leaving them to the choosing of flowers and the careful cutting of stems, he turned on his heel and headed for Chloe's.

'Sam and Nico will be along soon,' he told Chloe when she opened the door to him. 'Thanks for the dinner invite.'

'What are they doing?' Chloe wanted to know.

'Just some business they had to take care of.'

'What *kind* of business?'

'Their business,' he said with a grin. 'Have a little faith, Chloe. Alternatively, have a glass of wine. You look like you could use one.' He handed her the half-full bottle the waiter had recorked for them at the taverna. 'From Nico. I'd have bought some too only no one lets me buy alcohol around here.'

Chloe smirked. 'So I've heard. The general consensus is that you're quite forward enough without it. Come through.' Stepping aside, she gestured for him to enter.

Serena was setting the table when he entered the kitchen and Pete felt something shift and fall gently into place at the sight of her performing that simple task. Mealtimes and the setting of the dinner table had been important to his family too, once upon a time. Before his mother had died. Before his father had fallen apart, leaving Jake, and him as next eldest, to step in and make sure that clothes got washed and people got fed. He'd been sixteen at the time, Jake had been eighteen, and they'd managed well enough. Managed just fine, considering…

But food had generally made it to a person's stomach directly from the fridge or by way of the kitchen counter. Food had rarely stopped by the dinner table *en route*. Not his choice. No one's choice really. That was just the way things had shaken down.

He'd grown used to eating meals on the run. To loading up a food tray in a Navy mess hall, or stopping for take-away on the way home from work. Food was fuel, no need to celebrate the eating of it.

Maybe that was why the simple act of Serena laying knives and forks on the table cut at him so deeply, reminding him of his mother and of family the way it should be.

Maybe that was why he crossed over to the domestic goddess, set his palms to her face and touched his lips to hers for a kiss that spoke of tenderness, and thanks, and a moment in time he wanted to cherish.

Serena's eyes fluttered closed and the cutlery she'd been holding clattered to the table as Pete's lips met hers. There was passion in his kiss; there always was. A lick of heat and a dash of recklessness that called to her and made her tremble. But this time his passion was tempered with sweetness and a longing she'd never felt from him before. This wasn't a hello kiss. It wasn't seduction.

This kiss was all about coming home.

'What was that for?' she said shakily when he finally released her.

'Would you believe for setting the dinner table?'

'Are you serious?'

He sent her his charming, reckless smile. 'Maybe.'

She narrowed her eyes, mulled over his words and cursed him for being so much more than she wanted him to be. 'You love the idea of coming home to this every night, don't you? Coming home to family. You're not a carefree playboy at all. You're a fraud!'

'Only lately. Sorry I interrupted.' He picked up the cutlery and dumped it back in her hand. 'Feel free to continue. You looked like you were enjoying it and Lord knows I'll enjoy watching you.'

'Don't get any ideas,' she snapped. 'I'm a career woman.'

His smile deepened. 'I know that.'

'Guess you're not the only fraud around here,' Chloe murmured to him as she handed him a glass of wine. Serena opened her mouth to protest, Chloe raised a delicate eyebrow and shoved a glass of wine in her free hand too. 'Watch her deny it,' she said to Pete.

'Just because I don't mind setting a dinner table doesn't mean I want a life of domestic servitude,' she muttered loftily, taking a sip of her wine before putting it down and carrying on with the task of laying out the cutlery.

'Just because I like watching you set a dinner table doesn't mean you couldn't chase your chosen career.' He leaned forward, battle ready, a blue-eyed black-haired thief of hearts who could have charmed the moon down from the sky if he put his mind to it. 'I'm quite capable of setting a table myself. Or not at all if it comes to that.'

'You were right,' Chloe told her from the counter, her movements deft and practised as she swiftly uncorked another bottle of wine. 'Standing here listening to you two argue about a simple everyday task that takes about two minutes is *so* much better than standing here brooding.'

Sam and Nico arrived not long after that, the latter with pink roses, white daisies and green ferny things in hand. 'Pretty,' said Serena as Nico handed them over to a suddenly tongue-tied Chloe. 'A man who can find flowers like that at this time of night is both romantic and resourceful.'

'Although not entirely discreet,' murmured Pete.

'He doesn't need to be discreet,' countered Serena. 'His intentions are pure.'

'Not that pure,' said Nico.

'What about honourable?' said Pete.

'They're mostly honourable,' said Nico.

Chloe glared at them both. 'Do you *mind*? There's a *child* present.'

Sam rolled his eyes, Pete grinned his sympathy. 'I just figured Sam should probably know the difference between courtship and seduction too. You know…for future reference. At first I thought it had something to do with speed, seduction being the faster of the two methods of wooing a woman. Then I got to thinking it might have something to do with a man's intentions, but, no, man's intentions are a grey area. Who in their right mind would base it on that?'

'A woman might,' said Nico. 'They get some strange notions in their heads at times.'

'You're right,' said Pete.

'Aren't they sweet?' said Serena. 'All that brawn, so little brain… Puts me in mind of Winnie the Pooh. He was a bear of little brain too.'

'But cuddly,' said Pete. 'Generally happy with his lot.'

'Well, that rules you out, flyboy,' she murmured, handing him a plate of food. 'You can't even *find* your lot.'

She was right. But it still stung. 'I'll know it when I see it,' he said defensively.

'It's in your folder,' she said dryly. 'Three pages in.'

Pete unwound over the course of the dinner, everyone did, with the help of Chloe's excellent cooking and hospitality skills and Serena's knack for turning conversation into entertainment. Caring bubbled beneath the surface; bonds of friendship and of blood; ties of affection and of love.

The ache around his heart was gone.

They didn't make it a late evening, what with early starts for him and Nico the following morning and Sam looking increasingly sleepy.

'Walk me to the door,' he murmured to Serena as Nico made his farewells to Chloe and Sam.

'I'm sorry the evening didn't quite go to plan,' Serena said to him when they reached Chloe's front step. 'It probably wasn't what you had in mind. It certainly wasn't what I had in mind.'

'I'm not unhappy with the way it turned out,' he told her.

'The lack of mind-blowing sex doesn't bother you?'

'Is this a trick question?' Because he didn't have the faintest idea how to answer it.

'No, it's just a regular question.'

He still didn't know how to answer it. 'Hell, Serena.' He opted for the simple unvarnished truth. 'I just wanted to see you again.'

'Are you courting me, Pete Bennett?'

'Damned if I know.' He thought he might be. He thought he might just keep that bit of information to himself.

'When are you leaving in the morning?' she asked.

'Early.'

'When will you be back?'

'Soon. Alternatively, you could come up with another reason to get off this island. You could come with me in the morning.'

'You *do* miss the mind-blowing sex!'

Pete reached out to run a wayward strand of her hair through his fingers, noting with interest the way her eyes seemed to darken at his nearness and his touch. 'Maybe a little.' Maybe he wasn't the only one.

'The need is there, don't get me wrong,' she told him. 'But practically speaking it's just not possible to get away right now. I have Nico and Chloe to throw together…Vespa hire to arrange so I don't let my grandparents down. How about we aim to meet up in Athens in a few days' time?'

'We can do that,' he said. And with more bravado than sense, 'It doesn't bother you that I had to come and see you tonight?'

'Should it?' she whispered, her eyes dark and fey.

'I don't know,' he muttered. 'But it sure as hell bothers me.'

'Where's Nico?' Serena asked Chloe when she came back into the kitchen. 'And Sam?'

'Nico's gone to talk to Theo about fish-hooks for tomorrow,' said Chloe. 'I dare say he'll also find a way to casually mention that dinner's over, Pete's back in his hotel room, and that you and he are about to head back to the cottage. He'll be back in a few minutes. Sam's putting the rubbish out.'

Serena started stacking plates in the dishwasher while Chloe found containers for the remaining food.

'I was watching you with Pete Bennett tonight,' said Chloe, uncharacteristically hesitant. 'He's more than passing fond of you, Serena.'

Serena shook her head. 'He's playing a game, that's all. And he's very, very good at it.'

'Maybe he is,' murmured Chloe. 'Maybe that's exactly what he's doing. But for what it's worth I think you should start thinking about what you're going to do if he ever decides to stop.' Sam swung in through the back door and Chloe turned towards him. 'Thank you, Sam.'

Sam shrugged awkwardly.

'Had enough to eat?' Chloe said next.

He nodded.

'Then it's bedtime.' Chloe paused awkwardly. 'Would you like me to come up with you?'

'I'm not *six*,' he said scathingly, shooting her a dark glare before scooping up his schoolbooks and heading from the room.

'I thought things were improving,' said Serena into the silence Sam left in his wake.

'They are. This is one of our better days,' said Chloe with a strangled laugh. 'I don't know how to help him, Rena. He wants nothing from me. He's so defensive. So fiercely independent.'

'Maybe he's had to be,' she said gently. 'It can't have been easy looking after his mother.' Watching her die.

'I know.' Tears welled in Chloe's eyes. 'I hate the thought of it. There was no *need* for it. One phone call from my sister, one single phone call, and I'd have been there. She *knew* that, but no. She was too proud for that; too damn selfish. Even if she wanted nothing for herself why didn't she ask it for Sam, Serena? Why? What kind of mother makes an eleven-year-old bear the brunt of her illness alone?'

There was a slight shuffling noise in the doorway and Serena turned just in time to see Sam's retreating form. Her stomach clenched. The kitchen and dining area was a large one. The doorway stood a fair distance away. He probably hadn't heard them. And yet…

'He heard us.'

'No,' Serena muttered, desperately trying to believe it. 'He was too far away. And even if he did hear us, we didn't say anything wrong.'

'I criticised my sister.' Chloe's eyes were like bruises. 'I shouldn't have done that, even if I believed it. Not in front of Sam.'

'He didn't hear you.' Serena held Chloe's panicked gaze with her own. 'He couldn't have,' she said firmly. And prayed that it was so.

CHAPTER NINE

THERE was something to be said for sitting beneath a stripy blue beach umbrella next to a little tin shed half full of Vespas and dreaming about a man. It helped pass the time, decided Serena. It kept a brain agile and a body…aware. The breeze playing with her hair put her in mind of Pete's hands in it, the sun on her skin reminded her of the warmth of his body. She wanted to be back in his arms. Soon. That was a given. The trick lay in figuring out how to get there without disgracing her family in the process.

Nico delivered her lunch a little later than usual. He looked tired, subdued. As if he carried the weight of the world on his shoulders and then some. But he handed her the day's mail and her lunchbox, same as usual, and hunkered down in the chair beside her.

'Chloe was waiting down at the docks when the boats came in this morning,' he said finally.

That sounded promising. 'Moon kissed roses will do that to a girl.'

'Sam's not at school.'

That didn't sound promising at all.

'She thought he might have been waiting for the boats to come in. Waiting for me. He wasn't.'

'Oh.'

'Chloe told me what she'd said about his mother. She thinks Sam overheard her.' He ran a hand through his already untidy hair. 'Some of his clothes are gone. His wallet…Chloe thinks *he's* gone.'

'Gone where?'

Nico shrugged helplessly. 'I checked the ferry terminal, the ticket office. He didn't buy a ticket off the island, no one saw him getting onto a ferry. Chances are he's somewhere on the island. I thought I'd take a Vespa out and look around. He's probably just gone for a swim, or a walk. He does that sometimes. Skips out for a while. That's probably all that's happened.'

Serena nodded. 'Yeah. He'll be around.' She looked up at the hill, looked out over the sea. 'Where could he go?'

By mid-afternoon all the Vespas bar the one Nico had taken out were back in the shed. None of Serena's customers had seen Sam; *no one* had seen Sam, according to Chloe, and Serena had decided to shut up shop for the rest of the day.

Chloe was helping her.

When Nico rode up and told them his sea catamaran was missing, Chloe's face crumpled. Nico watched in silence, his own face a study in indecision before finally he reached out and drew Chloe into his arms.

'Not quite the way I imagined it,' he murmured softly to Chloe. 'Not quite the reason why.'

Chloe laughed through her tears, a choked, strangled sound, and her arms tightened around him.

'You think Sam's taken it out?' Serena asked him quietly.

'It's too big for him, Serena. If he tips it he'll never get the sail back up.' Nico looked out to sea. 'The wind's blowing North East. I'll take Theo's speedboat out. If Sam *has* taken the cat he won't have got far.' He rattled off Theo's radio frequency, Serena wrote it on her hand. She wrote it on Chloe's hand too, the one still wrapped around her cousin.

'I'm coming with you,' Chloe told Nico shakily.

'No.' He set her away and smoothed the hair from her face with gentle hands. 'You keep looking for him here. Keep asking around. Get Marianne Papadopoulos onto it.'

'I've already called her,' mumbled Chloe. 'I've called everyone on the island. There's no one left to call.'

Maybe not on *this* island. Serena pulled out her cell phone and started scrolling through her directory for a newly familiar number. Nico's gaze sought hers as she put the phone to her ear and he gave her the tiniest of nods. He already knew where her thoughts were headed. She was calling Pete.

'Where are you?' she said when he answered the phone.

'Kos,' he said cheerfully. 'Tell me you're about to walk through this restaurant door in a sky-blue sundress and make my day.'

'Sam's missing,' she said baldly.

Silence from Pete's end, silence from hers while she waited for him to comprehend the situation and change direction. He did it in a heartbeat, moving smoothly from lover to warrior and earning her undying admiration in the process. 'Have you reported it to the authorities?'

'Chloe's doing it now. He hasn't been gone all that long, only a few hours, but Chloe's worried about him. We all are.' She gave him the worst of it. 'Nico's super-cat is missing too.'

'Where's Nico?'

'On his way to the harbour. He's taking Theo's speedboat out to look around.'

'What's his radio frequency?'

She gave it to him, along with Nico's mobile number.

'Give him mine,' said Chloe anxiously, and she gave him that too.

'Pete—'

'Keep in contact with Nico,' he said. 'Try and contact some of the other boats you know are in the area. Ferries, fishing boats, charter boats. Concentrate on finding that cat.'

'How soon can you get here?' She wanted him here. *Needed* him here. They all did.

'Soon.'

Serena had never felt more at a loss for direction in her life. She and Chloe had taken a Vespa and scoured the nearby beaches for Sam but they'd seen no sign of him and after an hour of fruitless searching they'd decided to head for the village and for Marianne Papadopoulos's shop. The older woman had the best gossip network on the island, they reasoned. If anyone could get people mobilised and out looking for Sam, she could.

She did. With efficiency more suited to a general than a baker Marianne Papadopoulos assembled her ranks, appointed her colonels and set them loose. Theo would contact all the vessels in the area. Other key people would organise land search parties if Sam didn't show up soon. It was still early, she told Chloe gently. If Sam was on the island they'd find him. If he'd taken to the sea then Nico would find him. She didn't say what they were all thinking. That for a city boy like Sam, the sea was a dangerous place and that if something happened to him out there they might never find him.

It was a big sea.

Chloe was too tense to eat; Chloe existed on coffee. Serena bypassed the coffee in favour of cake. Each to their own.

It was Marianne Papadopoulos who first heard the helicopter coming in.

'You called Tomas's pilot?' she asked Serena bluntly. 'The one you've been stringing along these past few weeks?'

'Not stringing along,' she said defensively. 'Getting to know, and, yes, I called him.'

'Good girl,' said Marianne. 'Here he comes now.'

'Time to go,' Serena told Chloe, wresting the half full cup of coffee from Chloe's fingers and setting it on the counter. 'Pete's here.' And to the older woman, 'You have our numbers? You have Nico's?'

'You just get me your young man's radio contact details and I'll have them all,' said Marianne and handed her a cake box. 'For when you get hungry,' she said. 'For when you need hope.'

* * *

'Have you found him?' were Pete's first words as he stepped out of the helicopter.

Serena shook her head.

'I need to refuel,' were his second. 'We'll be in the air in five minutes. Get in.' He was all business, but he had a kiss for Chloe's forehead as he saw her seated in the rear of the cockpit and a smile for Serena as he pointed her to the seat beside him in the front. 'I'm glad you called,' he said.

'I'm glad you came.'

'Who's your ground-crew co-ordinator?'

'Marianne Papadopoulos. She wants your contact details.'

'She'll get them. I've already spoken to Nico. He's concentrating his search in the North Eastern corridor. We'll broaden ours.'

He radioed Mrs P, gave Serena a map and told her to grid it up. He got them airborne, explained the search pattern they'd use and told them how best to scour the sea below them without courting excess eyestrain and fatigue. He kept positive, kept Chloe calm, kept them looking. With cool deliberation Pete Bennett, air-sea rescue helicopter pilot, took charge.

Serena had never seen anything more beautiful in her entire life.

They searched for what felt like for ever, until the little helicopter needed to refuel. He sent them to the bathroom when they landed, made them drink and eat cake while he arranged with Theo to find spotlights, searchlights he could attach to the helicopter when they refuelled next. If they didn't find Sam soon, they'd be searching in the dark.

With just over two hours of daylight left he took them up again.

Serena shaded in more little boxes on the map on her knees and scoured the water below them for some sign of Nico's catamaran, some sign of Sam. But they didn't find either.

The wind blew stronger as the day wore on. Tiny whitecaps formed on top of the waves and the light started to fade, making searching for things like small boys alone in the water harder. Serena's eyes felt dry and gritty but she didn't stop looking. No one did.

It felt like hours later when Chloe spoke up. 'There,' she said, her voice thready with fatigue. 'There's something over there.' There being over to the west, straight into the sun. The *something* that Chloe was referring to being a white speck that Serena had to strain to see.

'I see it,' said Pete, and something in his voice made Serena sit up straighter and catch her breath as they changed course, dipping lower as they sped towards that speck of white. He was on the radio to Nico, relaying coordinates, almost before Serena could make out the shape of a sail in the water and a small figure clinging to an overturned catamaran hull.

'It's him. We found him!'

Pete smiled grimly. 'Yeah, but we still can't *get* to him.'

'He's not moving,' said Chloe, panic lacing her voice as she fumbled with her seat harness. 'He's hurt. His head's all bloody!'

Pete brought the chopper in for a closer look, balancing their need to know more with Sam's need to stay clinging to that hull. The noise should have roused the boy; the spray kicked up by the hovering helicopter should have done it… Not too close, not too close…

'His hand moved,' muttered Serena.

Not moved, thought Pete grimly. Slipped.

'He's letting go,' said Chloe, wrenching a life-jacket from beneath her seat and opening the door.

'What are you doing?' Pete swivelled round in his seat to glare at her.

'Chloe—' began Serena, unbuckling her own seat belt.

Chloe ignored them both, tugging the inflator tag on the lifejacket and hurling it out and down. Pete watched the life-jacket settle on the water a good fifty metres away from the target.

Chloe swore. Serena sought to calm her. 'Sam doesn't need it. He's got the hull. Nico'll get him.'

'Tell him to hurry,' said Chloe and disappeared out the door after the life jacket.

Pete felt the weight of the helicopter shift, adjusted for it, swinging high and wide and swearing long and loud as Chloe hit the water. 'Fifteen feet!' he raged. 'A swimmer jumps from fifteen feet, dammit!' Thirty feet and a body could break a leg. Fifty feet and people started dying. 'Where is she? Where the *hell* is she?' Had she gone in feet first? The clearance between the door and the rotor blades on this thing was tiny. Had she crossed her arms as she'd gone out the door or flung them above her head? Hell! Did she have any arms *left*?

'It's okay.'

He wrestled with the helicopter, got it back where he

wanted it, off to one side of where Chloe had gone in and far enough away from Sam so as not to disturb his hold on the hull. He looked back to find Serena hanging out the door, looking for Chloe, and his heart did stop. 'Get back in the cockpit,' he roared. 'So help me, Serena, if you follow her I'll kill you myself!' His words were drowned by the thumping of the rotor blades but she heard him, looked back at him, her hair flying about her face as she grinned at him.

'I'm not!' she roared back. 'She's okay. She's got the lifejacket!'

'She'd have had it to start with if she'd put it *on* before she *jumped*!' He longed for a Seahawk, and a crew. Sean running the winch and Merry in the water. A safety line and a basket, *some* damn way of getting Sam—and now Chloe—into the helicopter and headed for land, but a man made do with what he had and got on the radio and told Nico that there were two in the water now and to get a move on.

Nico's savage curses echoed his feelings perfectly. The other man didn't need to ask who else was in the water and Pete had no mind to tell him. The two most important people in the world to Nico were down there—he'd get there as fast as he could.

'It's all right,' muttered Serena, putting her hand to his shoulder as she climbed back through to the front and settled into the seat beside him. 'Chloe's a good swimmer. A good sailor. She'll right that cat and sail it if she has to. Where's Nico? How far away?'

'He'll be here,' he told her and edged the helicopter higher and wider so as not to impede Chloe's passage to the catamaran. She was almost there, was there, and he watched in grim satisfaction as she hauled herself up on the hull, straddled it and put the lifejacket on before edging towards Sam. Finally some sea craft and some sense.

'Look,' said Serena in a choked voice and he watched as Chloe inched towards the boy, talking to him, all the time talking to him, as tears coursed down her face. Sam's eyes fluttered open, and his hand moved towards her, just a fraction. And then Chloe was hauling him onto the hull, gathering him up in her arms and he was clinging to her as if he'd never let go. 'It's going to be all right. Chloe's got him. Look. She won't let go.'

Pete nodded curtly, not wanting to tell her that it was far from okay. They didn't know how bad Sam's head wound was—whether it was just a bump or if he'd done some real damage. He didn't want to remember the times when not letting go simply hadn't been enough to see a soul through. Not this time, he prayed to whatever God cared to listen. Please, not this time.

He manoeuvred the helicopter higher. There was nothing they could do but give Chloe and Sam smoother seas and less noise. Nothing to do but lift that bird higher so that Nico could see them; so that they could see him coming. He radioed Marianne and the authorities, arranged for the doctor to be waiting when Nico brought them in. There was nothing left to do.

He waited until Nico appeared on the horizon, skimming across the water in Theo's speedboat like a low-flying bullet. He kept the Jet Ranger hovering until Nico reached them. Watched as Sam's arms suddenly found strength and he clung to Chloe until finally, finally Nico persuaded him to let her go.

When Nico had settled Chloe in the speedboat with Sam back in her arms and blankets around them both, Pete turned to Serena and smiled his relief.

Mindless of the throttle and the controls she covered his face, his cheek, his hair with kisses and promptly burst into tears.

When her tears and her kisses had diminished somewhat he ordered her back in her seat and finally headed for land.

The locals who had joined in the land search for Sam had already gathered in Chloe's taverna by the time Pete and Serena stepped into the hotel a good half an hour after landing. He accepted the beer Theo and Marianne Papadopoulos set in front of him with a grin, accepted the congratulations they offered, but he wasn't quite ready to celebrate, not yet.

Yes, they'd found Sam, but until a doctor or a medic had checked the boy over and cleared him of serious injury Pete's celebrations would remain subdued.

Serena sat beside him at the bar, her eyes weary but her smile impish. They'd bought her a beer too. 'We found him,' she said as she touched her glass to his. 'Cheer up, flyboy. Smile a little.'

He smiled a little. 'It's a start.'

'It's a good start,' she corrected him.

More locals filtered into the room, drawn by shared concern and hope of good news. This was a tight-knit community and for tonight at any rate they were willing to let him be part of it. They knew who he was. They congratulated him on his efforts and on finding Sam.

'It's my job,' he started to say more than once, only that was a lie and he refused to be caught in it. He wasn't an air-sea rescue pilot any more. He didn't know what he was.

He wanted to know how serious the boy's injuries were. He wanted the relief that would come with knowing that Sam was going to be fine. *Then* he could celebrate.

Serena's phone rang and she covered her free ear from the din as she took the call, leaning forward, resting her elbows on the bar.

'Shh,' said Marianne, her eyes as sharp as ever and her senses honed for gossip. 'Shh!'

The crowd quietened a little, not a lot, and Pete placed his hand on the small of Serena's back, seeking her warmth, offering his. The eyes of the crowd were upon them this night but he didn't care what gossip might come of his actions. Serena mattered to him; her happiness and her future mattered to him. So did Sam's.

He was through with being discreet.

He leaned forward, his brow almost touching hers as she tucked a thick fall of hair behind her ear with shaking fingers before seeking his free hand with hers, twining her fingers through his and holding on tight. 'They're back,' she whispered. 'Sam's with the doctor now. Nico says he's talking, that his eyes are clear and that the cut on his head doesn't look that big now that they've cleared most of the blood away.' Her eyes sought his, filling with tears. 'Nico says the doctor says he's fine!'

She stood up abruptly, repeated her words in Greek

and the crowd erupted. People started kissing him, his face, his hair, and somehow he was standing and Serena was kissing him too.

The mood really turned celebratory after that and by the time Nico and Chloe walked in, Nico carrying a drowsy boy with a big sunburn and a mercifully little bandage on his head, it was standing room only. The three of them stayed a few minutes, just long enough for Sam to receive the kissing treatment and Chloe to thank everyone for their help and declare drinks on the house. And then, stating firmly that Sam needed to rest, all three of them made their escape.

Pete stayed long enough to collect more congratulations, stayed long enough to see Serena drawn into the laughing crowd, part of it in a way he would never be, before he too took his leave.

Serena knew it the minute he left. She thought he'd be back. That maybe he'd gone to check in. He was hero of the hour and he'd been enjoying it, she could have sworn he had, but as twenty minutes slipped by and then another twenty and he still hadn't returned, Serena began to doubt that he would. Would he leave without telling her?

She didn't know.

He'd seemed subdued. Even after seeing Sam, talking to him, and telling Chloe to never *ever* jump out of his helicopter like that again, he'd been subdued. Adrenalin was a funny beast. Hours later her body still thrummed with it. The air tasted sharper, the lights shone brighter. She was hyper alert, almost bursting out of her skin with energy. Did he feel that way too? The bulk of the decision-making regarding the search had rested with him these past few hours. Did he feel *more*?

How the hell did a person handle more adrenalin than *this*?

She checked with Reception only to find that he'd booked a room but wasn't in it. She checked with Chloe and Nico but he wasn't there either. She walked outside, her eyes drawn to the track that led up to her grandparents' cottage and beyond.

She looked to the sky and thought she knew where she might find him.

Serena stopped off at the cottage on her way. She needed a jacket against the coolness of the night air, never mind that her walk up the hill would conceivably keep her warm. She grabbed the lightweight blanket at the foot of her bed at the last minute, and, trusting to moonlight rather than a torch she set off up the goat track.

She found him on the plateau, with the lights of the village spread out below him and the stars shining above. She dumped the blanket at his feet and waited for him to speak.

He looked at the blanket, looked at her, and the faintest of smiles crossed his lips.

'Is that a hint?' he said.

'You left early.'

He shrugged. 'I'd had enough.'

'You don't like it when people honour you?'

'I like it well enough.'

'So why leave?' Why leave without *me*? was what she meant.

He looked at her, his eyes dark and unfathomable. 'I'm tired, Serena. I couldn't think back there. And I needed to.'

He was thinking about other rescues, other times when his best just hadn't been enough. She could see it in his eyes.

'You were wonderful today. You know that, don't you?'

He shrugged. 'It's a situation I'm familiar with. It's just training.'

'Then I'm glad you chose to undertake it.' She took a deep breath. 'I watched you today. Watched you come alive in a way I've never seen before. Watched you be what I've always known you could be. It was a beautiful thing. Made me realise something I think you already know in your heart.' She moved forward to cup his cheek, drawing his gaze to hers. 'You don't belong here, Pete Bennett. Flying tourists around these islands or mustering cattle or hauling cargo or whatever else it is you think you might do next. People need those skills you've learned. The air-sea rescue service needs them. Go home.'

'That's your advice?'

'Well, yeah. I realise it's a little short on ways to manage those feelings that made you run in the first place, but I'm working on that.'

'You are?' He smiled a crooked smile. 'Let me know how it goes.'

She planned to. 'I know it gets personal when you don't save a soul. It cuts deep. Because you care. Because failure isn't an option for you when it comes to saving lives.'

'It's an option, Serena. It's a reality.'

'I know. But when you're up there searching for someone it's not *your* reality. Not until death rams it down your throat.'

He didn't disagree with her. Couldn't, she thought with an ache in her heart. 'Ask me why I called you when Sam went missing.'

'Because you needed a helicopter?' He brushed her cheek with the back of his knuckles, gentle, so very gentle for a man with such strength.

'Because we needed *you*. Because you care. Because failure just isn't an option for you when it comes to saving lives. It's quite a conundrum you've got there, flyboy. Because if you didn't feel the loss of the people you couldn't save quite so keenly you wouldn't be nearly as good at saving the ones you do.'

'That's not advice, Serena. It's a summary.'

She had to laugh at the stubborn jut of his chin, had to step in closer and set her lips to it. 'All I'm saying is that if you accept the bad as a necessary part of the work you do, it might not weigh so heavy on your soul.' Now *that* was advice. Whether or not he would take it was anyone's guess.

'I'll think about it later.' His eyes darkened as his gaze came to rest on her lips. 'I'm thinking about something else right now.'

'Oh?' Her hands settled on his shoulders. So much strength in this man, so much heat. 'What might that be?'

'You.'

'Excellent. Because I'm hoping you'll give *me* some advice. Happens I find myself standing here with an overabundance of energy I can't seem to get rid of.'

'Leftover adrenalin.' His lips brushed hers, lingering, promising, dragging gently and setting her nerves on fire. 'You need to give it direction.'

'I'm so glad you agree.' She set her lips to his for a hot, open-mouthed kiss and directed it, all of it, straight at him.

He wasn't prepared for it. He hadn't realised just how fast she could ignite his passion and rouse his hunger. Too much. More than he could handle and still be careful of her. And still he let his need for her come and when it did he feared it and gloried in it in turn as her mouth played his; hot, soft, knowing.

'Slow down,' he murmured as sensation crashed over him like a wave, dragging at his control, trying to wrest it from him. 'Please, Serena. Slow down.'

'Can't,' she muttered. 'There's only you, only this. Help me.'

But her words had pushed him beyond helping anyone.

He fisted his hand in her hair and tugged, exposing her neck to his lips, grazing her collar bone with his teeth not nearly as lightly as he would have wished. He found the throbbing pulse at the base of her neck, tasted salt on his tongue as she threaded her hands in his hair, tilted her head back and offered up more.

He wanted to savour her, to take his time, but his hands rushed down her back, over her curves, and his grip turned hard and biting as he dragged her lower body against his. 'I'm sorry,' he muttered as he surged against her, but she didn't seem to mind at all.

'The blanket,' she muttered as she writhed against him, her fingers dealing swiftly with the buttons of his shirt.

He backed off, letting her go long enough to find it and spread it out before reaching for her again and dragging her to the ground. He wanted her on her back, naked and open. That was the start of it. Heaven only knew where his hunger would take them after that. He fumbled with the buttons at the front of her dress. No, not a button, it was a snap. He tugged. One snap. Two. A flurry of snaps as she shrugged out of the dress altogether and she was lying down, her eyes not leaving his face as she crossed her wrists above her head and offered her body to him and the night, to the sky, like some pagan goddess.

'I don't want to hurt you.' It was a plea, a warning, and came straight from his soul. His hands were at her hips, on her thighs, too rushed, too needy. Just like his mouth as it followed his hands, teasing, biting, ravenous.

'You won't,' she whispered, and with a ragged oath he pushed her thighs wide open and set his mouth to her.

Serena bucked beneath the lash of his tongue and the wild desire that speared her body. Her hands fisted and she cried out, a high keening sound that spoke of a pleasure so intense it bordered on pain, but she did not make him stop. And that hungry, knowing mouth drove her higher and higher with ruthless precision. Too fast, but she couldn't slow down, too much and still she ached for more. She was out of control, out of her depth with this man, but she didn't care. She needed him. And then climax ripped through her and Serena closed her eyes as need vanished beneath the onslaught of outrageous, all-consuming pleasure.

He was looming over her when finally she surfaced, his hair mussed, and his eyes sharp with desire. She murmured her approval as he shed his shirt but it wasn't enough. 'I want more,' she muttered, her hands moving down the taut planes of his stomach towards the huge, hard bulge in his trousers.

'How much more?'

'All.' She undid his trouser buttons and then his fly. Pushed them down his legs until he was as naked as she was. 'Everything.'

His curse was succinct. Appropriate. He sheathed himself inside her with one smooth stroke and she cried out at the urgency and the wildness in him. He rolled onto his back, dragging her with him and she rode him, blind with need, her body demanding its due as she took him deep inside her, until there was nothing between them, not even moonlight.

'No,' he whispered as he started to move, ragged strokes to match his breathing, every magnificent line of him radiating tension. 'Not all. Not everything. I can't.'

But he did.

With every fierce caress, he gave it. With every shudder of his body he showed it.

'You and me, Pete Bennett. Whatever you want. Whatever you need from me. Take it.' She was spiralling out of control, tightening around him, moments away from orgasm. 'Because heaven help me I'm going to take what I need from you.'

'All right,' he muttered and it was both a curse and a prayer. 'All right, then.' His lips crushed down on hers, drinking her in, driving her insane. 'Together.'

* * *

He honoured his word. In the lovemaking that followed they reached the stars together. He honoured his word in the way he roused her from sleep at dawn and pulled her against him; back to front, like spoons in a drawer as they watched the sun rise from the ocean.

Serena watched, breathless, until the sun gained its freedom from the water and then she rolled over onto her back and looked her fill at another view just as breathtaking. The sunrise had held a soft and gentle beauty. The man leaning on his elbows staring down at her possessed a different kind of beauty, his face all angles and planes, his mouth straight and unsmiling. She looked to his eyes, unprepared for the utter bleakness she saw in their depths. And then he smiled and his eyes warmed.

'I want my camera,' she murmured.

'For the sunrise?'

'For you.' She breathed deep to catch his scent. 'You're magnificent. When you smile you fill my heart. When you're solemn you damn near break it.' She couldn't get enough of this man. Every time she touched him, kissed him, made love to him, she wanted more.

He ran a hand through his hair and sat upright, taking most of the blanket with him.

'Places to go, flyboy?'

'Exactly. Not to mention someone else's business to run.'

'Does that mean that if it were *your* business you'd be inclined to linger?'

'Probably. You do strange things to my perception of what's important. Now get up.'

Pleasure warred with indignation. Pleasure won as

she trailed a finger down his back. 'Five more minutes,' she said.

'No.'

She trailed a finger up his back, pleased when he shuddered beneath her touch. 'Four and a half.'

He turned swiftly, pinning her to the ground, his eyes stormy but his touch gentle. 'Three,' he said gruffly.

But he gave her ten.

'What's your current position on discretion?' Pete asked her as they staggered down the hill towards the cottage. He needed coffee, food, and a scalding shower, all of which could be found at the hotel if his knees would carry him that far. Right now he was aiming for the cottage.

'I'm thinking it's a lost cause.' She stumbled over a rock, cursed as she got her feet beneath her and kept moving. 'Nico's at work. Or should be. There's food at the cottage. Coffee,' the word was almost a whimper. 'Fresh clothes.'

'I'll take the food and the coffee,' he muttered. 'Keep the clothes. Put them on. *Keep* them on.'

'Good idea.'

They all but fell into the kitchen and Serena headed straight for the fridge and a tin of fresh coffee beans that she dumped, double strength, into the coffee-maker before shoving a mug beneath the spout and turning it on. Civilisation poured into the cup, hissing and steaming, bringing with it rational thought and a groan of pure appreciation.

Breakfast began to happen in front of his eyes; a skillet full of sausages and tomatoes, bread in the toaster, another pan of eggs. 'Is that enough?' she wanted to know. 'It doesn't look like enough.'

'It's enough.' Never half measures with Serena, not in anything. He loved that about her. Despaired of it.

'Where will you be today?' she asked, keeping it casual, keeping it light, but he was fresh out of casual. He'd tried to play it her way this morning, tried to play the game, but his heart wasn't in it and therein lay the crux of the problem. His heart lay elsewhere.

'Kos.'

'You're going back to collect your passengers from yesterday?'

'Yes.'

She shot him a wary glance before taking a quick sip of her coffee. He had that grim look about him again. The one that said don't push me, don't poke, but she wasn't. Was she?

She'd been doing her utmost to pretend that the events of yesterday and last night hadn't shaken her to the core. Seeing firsthand his compassion and his strength. Demanding it for Sam, watching him deliver, and even after the job was done she hadn't had the courtesy to leave well enough alone. Rearranging his life for him, telling him where she thought he belonged, never mind his own thoughts on the matter. She didn't even know what his thoughts on the matter were.

'About what I said last night…' she muttered awkwardly.

He regarded her coolly. 'You said a lot of things last night, Serena.'

'About your work.'

'What about it?'

'I mean, it's up to you. Why should I have a say in what you do?'

His lips twisted. 'Why indeed?'

He set his coffee down on the bench, took the tongs from her unresisting hand and set about turning the sausages she'd forgotten. 'It's all right, Serena,' he said quietly. 'You didn't say anything I wasn't already thinking.'

'So... You're going home?'

'Yes.'

Sausage fat spat in the pan as her conviction that he was doing the right thing warred with a piercing sense of loss. She summoned a smile. 'I'm glad for you. I think. When will you go?'

'As soon as I find a replacement pilot. It shouldn't be too hard to persuade someone to come fly around paradise for a few weeks.'

'No. No, it shouldn't.' The pain grew sharper and she tried to absorb it. She admired his decision to return to the world of air-sea rescue. Knew in her heart he belonged there. It was the thought of him leaving that hurt. She didn't think she'd be able to look at a blue summer sky without thinking of him, and that was bad because there were a lot of blue summer skies in a lifetime.

At least, there should be.

'I guess now's the time to start being all civilised and mature about you going one way and me going another,' she said, striving for lightness and failing miserably.

'No.'

'No?'

'I can't do it.' He doused the flame beneath the skillet and turned to face her, his expression grave. 'You asked for everything last night, Serena,' he said quietly. 'I gave it.'

He'd never done this before. He'd never been the one to ask for more than a casual relationship. But he was asking it now. 'I'm going home, Serena. I want you to come with me. Be with me.' There was no easy way to say it. 'Marry me.'

He'd shocked her. He could see it in her eyes, in the way she stood so utterly still. It was too soon in their relationship, he knew it, knew damn well he was rushing her. But he'd run out of time. There was no other way. 'I know the timing's bad. And the last thing I want to do is stand in the way of your dreams or your job opportunities. We can talk about it. Work something out.' His heart faltered at her continued silence. 'Serena, say something.'

'I—' She reached out towards him with her hand as if pleading for something, only he didn't know what. She already had all of him. He had nothing left to give.

He jammed his hands in his trouser pockets and took a deep breath as he turned to stare out the kitchen window at the sea beyond. 'Think about it,' he said gruffly. 'I have a home on the Hawkesbury, just north of Sydney. It's set in the hills overlooking the water. There's a jetty there. A boat. It's peaceful. Beautiful. A little bit like this place. With Sydney on the doorstep.' Why wasn't she saying anything? 'You could work if you wanted to. You could freelance from home. Commute to Sydney.

Whatever you'd prefer. We could get a bigger helicopter.' She hadn't moved since he'd started talking. She just stood there in silence. An ocean full of silence. So this was what it felt like to drown. '*Dammit*, Serena, say something!'

'Like what?' He turned his head to look at her and she stared back at him, her eyes blazing and her face palè. She looked tragically, heartbreakingly magnificent in her anger—if it was anger, she still hadn't said enough for him to be sure. Maybe it only looked like anger. But it sure as hell didn't look like joy. 'That you're tearing me in two? Well, you are!'

She put her hands to her head and stalked towards the table, turned and stalked back until she was level with him. 'I thought we agreed,' she said hotly. 'I thought we were playing. That we were *both* playing. You *know* this game, Pete Bennett. Don't you dare tell me you don't!'

'I know it,' he said quietly, while his heart shattered into pieces at her feet. 'I just can't play it any more. Not with you. I've never been able to play it right with you.'

'But you have to!' she said, her eyes filling with tears. 'You have to, don't you see? I got the Athens job. The one you helped me get.' And with a choking laugh, 'Damn you, Pete Bennett, I got the job!'

He watched her race across the kitchen and slam out the door, out of his sight.

So much for asking her to be his wife.

Guess that was a no.

CHAPTER TEN

BLEAK didn't begin to describe Serena's feelings. She couldn't understand how a day that had begun with such happiness and such promise had degenerated so swiftly into a day full of hurt and despair. Her fault, she knew it. She'd asked for too much, demanded all Pete had to give, craving it all, taking it all, and never realising that there would be a reckoning; that he would make her pay.

Bastard.

Anger took the edge off her misery, never mind that it was misdirected. It was there, inside her. No point wasting it. So she stewed and she brooded and by the time Nico found her at lunchtime, in her usual place beside the Vespa shed, she'd acquired a head full of steam and an ocean of resentment towards the traitorous, thieving marauder of hearts, Peter, *Superman, flyboy*, Bennett.

Nico looked tired but happy as he handed over her lunchbox and settled into the chair beside her. Nico— if the unlived-in state of the cottage this morning was any indication—had not made it home last night. Good for him. 'How's Sam?'

'He'll mend,' said Nico, opening her cooler and pinching one of her cans of cola.

'And Chloe?'

'She'll mend too once she stops blaming herself for what happened. She's fussing over Sam something awful.' The hint of a smile touched Nico's lips as he set the cola to his lips and drank deeply. 'He's letting her.'

'Good.' Good for all of them.

'Chloe said she saw Pete this morning before he left,' he continued with a studied casualness she didn't believe one little bit. 'She said if he looked any more miserable she'd have bundled him up next to Sam for the day and mollycoddled them both.'

Serena said nothing.

'She asked him when he'd be back,' said Nico. 'She wanted to thank him properly for what he did for Sam. Take him out for a meal or a drink. *Something.*' Nico slid her a sideways glance. 'He said he didn't know.'

Serena felt the tears start to well and blinked them away, grateful for the sunglasses that hid her eyes until Nico set his drink on the ground and gently removed her sunglasses from her face and left her defenceless.

'He hurt you.'

'No.' *Yes.* 'It's nothing.'

'Then why are you crying?'

'I'm not crying,' she muttered, dashing the tears from her cheeks. 'You just took the sunglasses away too soon, that's all.' She took a deep shuddering breath. 'Pete's heading back to Australia. To his old job with air-sea rescue.'

Nico studied her intently. 'So you're crying because he's leaving?'

'No.' *Yes.* 'He asked me to go with him. To marry him.'

'Oh.' Nico leaned forward, scratched his head, and developed a sudden fascination with the ground beneath his feet. 'I would speak with your father on Pete's behalf if you wanted me to. If you thought he might not approve.'

'That's not it.'

'Didn't think so,' he said, turning his face towards her, his eyes sharp and searching. 'You refused him.'

'Not exactly.' She hadn't meant to ask for everything. She really hadn't. She stared at Nico helplessly, not knowing how to explain. Not knowing where to start. 'I just—' She waved her hand in the air.

Nico sighed. 'Did you say yes?'

'No.'

'Trust me. You refused him.'

Serena felt the tears start to come again. 'I got the job in Athens.'

'Well…' he said, and followed up with a lengthy pause. 'Congratulations. But that doesn't necessarily mean you have to take it.'

'If I don't take it…if I don't step out on my own *now* I'll never know if I could have succeeded.'

'Women,' he muttered.

'You don't understand,' she said hotly. 'This was supposed to be my time. *Mine.* You don't know how long I've waited for it!'

'I do know,' he said gently. 'And it still *is* your time, Serena. There's just another offer on the table now, that's all.' He sent her a wry smile. 'All you have to do is decide which one you want to take.'

Pete stayed away from sleepy Greek islands and soul-stealing sirens for well over a week but he couldn't stay away from the island for ever. Not when passengers wanted to go there. Not when passengers wanted to be picked up from there and flown to Athens.

His one saving grace was that he knew who his passengers were and Serena wasn't one of them. It was Chloe and Sam.

Chloe greeted him like a long lost brother when he touched down, which was sweet of her. Sam greeted him with something akin to awe.

'Where do you want to sit?' he asked the boy as they headed towards the Jet Ranger. 'Front or back?' His gaze slid to Chloe, his eyes narrowed. 'Actually, you take the back. Last time your aunt was in the back of my helicopter she jumped *out* of it. And don't think I've forgiven you either,' he muttered to Chloe. 'The memory of it will haunt me to the day I die.'

Chloe sent him an angelic smile. 'I knew what I was doing.'

'You did not!'

'Did she really jump out of your helicopter?' said Sam.

'Yes.' He didn't want to think about it.

'Chloe says you found me.'

'It was a group effort. Chloe spotted you, Nico came and got you, Mrs Papadopoulos had people out looking for you.' He gauged Sam's readiness to hear what he had to say next. Thought the boy ready for it. 'Pretty stupid move, Sam.'

'I know.' Sam's thin frame stiffened but he held Pete's gaze. 'I'm sorry.'

'I'm glad.' Pete gestured for him to get in the helicopter, showed him how to buckle up, and where the life-jackets were. 'Where were you headed, anyway?'

'Athens.'

'Flying's faster.'

'Yeah, but I can't fly a helicopter.'

'You can't sail either, but did that stop you trying? No.'

Chloe giggled first. Sam grinned. 'I'm gonna learn to sail first. Then I'm gonna learn how to fly.'

'Why not?' said Pete. 'So why the trip to Athens today? Something special on?'

Sam's smile faltered. Chloe answered for him. 'It's an anniversary—of a kind. Sam's mother died a year ago. We have a visit to make.'

'My mother died when I was not much older than you,' Pete told the boy gently. 'I do the same. Every year. It helps you remember.'

They touched down in Athens without incident, Sam helping him secure the rotor blades as Chloe gathered up all their stuff. The boy looked edgy. Tense. But it was a big day for him. He had a right to be tense and Pete left him well enough alone.

Sam's hands went to his pockets, nothing untoward about that except that when he withdrew his hand he clutched two fifty euro notes in it. He held them out to Pete, his expression guarded. 'They're yours,' he said.

'Are you sure?'

Sam nodded jerkily. 'Nico and Chloe are getting married. Nico says he's going to adopt me so that we'll all belong to each other. Like a family.' The wonder in Sam's eyes pierced Pete to the core.

'Take care of them, Sam,' he said gruffly.

'I will.' The words were a promise. Sam held out the money. 'Here. It's yours. I don't need them any more.'

Chloe had more words for him as they walked across the tarmac to the arrivals building.

'Serena left the island last week,' she told him.

Pete said nothing.

'She's staying with Nico's family while she tries out this new job. She has a two-week trial period.'

Pete shrugged. 'She won't need it. Her work is brilliant.'

'I hear she's conflicted,' said Chloe. 'She had another offer on the table that was tempting.'

Pete smiled bitterly. 'Congratulations on your engagement.'

'You're changing the subject,' she said.

'Yeah.'

'We're meeting her for coffee later. Care to join us?'

'No.'

'No message for her?'

'Yeah.' Pete's gut clenched. He'd never known how hard it was to be the one letting go. 'Tell her I'm proud of her.'

'You've seen Pete?' said Serena as Chloe gave Sam the okay to go and check out the pastries in the cabinet.

They were sitting in a café in Athens before Chloe and Sam headed back to Sathi. The question revealed more than it should but Serena asked it anyway.

'Of course I've seen him,' said Chloe. 'He flew us here. He's flying us back.'

'What did he look like? How did he seem?'

'He looked the way he always looks. Heartbreakingly handsome. He seemed fine.'

'Bastard,' she muttered.

'You, on the other hand, look miserable.'

'I'm not miserable. I'm fine.'

'How's the job going? Is it as fulfilling as you expected?'

'I've only been there a week,' she said dryly. 'Fulfilment takes time.'

'If you ask me, without the right man at your side, fulfilment's going to take for ever,' muttered Chloe. 'Not that you asked.'

'Since when did you become the expert?'

'Since your cousin asked me to marry him,' said Chloe shyly, and lifted her hand to display the sweetest diamond ring.

'Really?' A smile began to bloom deep in Serena's heart. Finally, something that was going right. 'I knew it,' she said as she leaned over and hugged Chloe tight. 'I knew it!' She sat back and beamed. 'He'll bring you laughter and happiness.'

'And fish,' said Chloe with a grin.

'And children,' said Serena, slanting a glance at Sam who was still glued to the sweets counter, seemingly unable to make a decision about which one to have.

'More children. You'll have a good life together, Chloe. I can feel it.'

'You could have had a good life too,' said Chloe quietly. 'With Pete.'

'I know.' Serena looked away.

'Call him,' said Chloe.

'And say what? Don't go back to Australia? Stay in Athens and cart tourists around for a living? It won't satisfy him, Chloe. I can't ask it of him.'

'Maybe he could get air-sea rescue work here. Have you asked him that? No. Have you discussed the possibility of you getting the kind of work you want back in Australia? No. You took the first job offered, and sold yourself short.'

'I had to start somewhere,' she said defensively.

'Don't get me started,' said Chloe curtly. 'Your photographs are wasted on a daily newspaper. Your pictures don't need words. You're an artist. That your family didn't encourage you in that direction long ago is shameful, but enough about my feelings on that.' She cut off her words with an abrupt wave of her hand. 'If you want to be a photojournalist, fine. Be one. But why on earth do you have to be one *here*?'

'It's not just that,' she said doggedly. 'I know it sounds selfish but I wanted to concentrate on me for a while. My wants. My wishes. My career. If I'd met him a few years from now it might have been different… *Would* have been different,' she admitted. 'I'd have been ready for what he offered me, Chloe, but right now I just don't know. Sometimes I want him with me so bad I ache. But I want my freedom too.'

'Marriage isn't a cage,' said Chloe, and held up her hands when Serena would have protested. 'Okay, I know it brings with it responsibilities and duty to other people. It brings complications when it comes to working out whose wants and needs should take priority. It can bring sacrifice and heartache, children to love, relatives to worry about, and more ties than you know what to do with and they just keep coming until they're wrapped around you like a cloak. But it's a cloak of gold, Serena—rich with dreams and with wishes, full of strength and of joy. It'll keep you warm in the winter and it'll be there for you to come home to after a hard day's work taking pictures that break your heart. It'll keep you strong for when you come home to a man who's been up in the sky all day scouring raging seas for non-existent survivors. Talk all you want about freedom, Serena, but what you found with Pete Bennett? It's worth something.'

'I know,' she said quietly.

'He said to tell you he's proud of you,' said Chloe.

Serena swallowed hard. Nodded. She couldn't speak.

'Do you love him?'

Serena nodded again.

'I can't tell you what to do, Serena, but if you love him the way he loves you?' Chloe smiled gently. 'It's worth everything.'

Serena stewed over her options another week before finally gathering the nerve to call Pete. Her two weeks trial working period was up. She'd found the work sat-isfying, occasionally exhilarating, and the deadlines tight. They were happy with her work. *She* was happy with it. Time to start looking for an apartment and carving out a life for herself in Athens if that was what she wanted.

But it wasn't.

She wanted something else more.

She needed to find out if it was still on offer. With shaking hands she reached for her phone. A recorded message told her his phone was out of range. She called the helicopter charter service. Tomas answered.

'How's the new job?' he wanted to know.

'It's a good job. Tomas, is Pete around?'

'Didn't he tell you?' said Tomas. 'His old air-sea rescue unit were desperately short a helicopter pilot. He's back in Australia. He went home.'

CHAPTER ELEVEN

THE plane from Athens, by way of Paris and Singapore, touched down in Sydney early Saturday morning, not quite one week after Serena's conversation with Tomas. The newspaper job had been a good one but in the end she'd respectfully declined it. She would find something closer to home, closer to where her heart was. Serena looked to the sky, such a bright and vivid blue sky, as she made her way from the arrivals terminal to a waiting taxi and told the driver to take her to a cityside hotel.

She needed to make plans before she tracked Pete Bennett down. She needed to figure out what to say and what to ask for. And what she would do if he turned her away.

She needed to try and ensure that didn't happen.

It was time to accessorise.

Pete Bennett was happy to be home. He'd slipped back into his old job as if he'd never left it: the training and the camaraderie, the Seahawks and the purpose behind it all. He was back, he was ready, and he had a newfound philosophy about dealing with the missions that didn't turn out the way he wanted them to. Whether that particular philosophy would work without Serena there to remind him of it was open to speculation.

He'd wondered about calling her before he left Greece. He could have asked her how the job was going, told her he was heading home. But in the end he hadn't called. He'd said everything he wanted to, offered everything he had, and she'd chosen not to take it.

There was nothing left to say.

So here he was, back in Sydney, back within reach of his family and all the stronger for it. His brothers were in town, all of them. Jake, who'd flown in from Singapore for reasons of his own that Pete had yet to fathom. Luke, who was home on shore leave. And Tristan, who lived here in Sydney these days. It wasn't often they were all together in the one place, it was something of an event and one that needed celebration.

Jake and Tristan had argued the where of it, but in the end they'd decided to take a trip down memory lane and spend the better part of this lazy Sunday afternoon at the local hotel down by the beach. Just like old times as Luke and Tristan started arguing the relative merits of different law enforcement agencies and Jake wheedled a set of darts from the barman and commandeered the dartboard. Home turf. There was no place quite like it for healing a wounded heart. No better company to do it in.

He'd get over her. He would.

Give it fifty, sixty, years he'd be just fine.

They paired up to play darts, him and Jake against Tristan and Luke. He liked darts. He could have whipped them all but for their incessant questions about Greece and beautiful women.

'So what does she do?' Luke asked him as he lined up his shot.

'Who?'

'The woman you left behind. The one who broke your heart.'

'Whatever she damn well wants,' he muttered, missing his mark by a good three centimetres.

'A wayward woman,' said Tristan. 'I like her already. Why didn't you bring her back with you?'

'Did you ask her?' said Luke curiously.

Pete glared at the pair of them. 'What is this? An inquisition?'

'Just curious,' said Luke. 'What are you going to do about her?'

'Nothing. She had another offer on the table. She took it. End of story.'

'What kind of offer?' asked Luke. 'An offer from another man? And you couldn't see it coming?'

'A job offer,' he said curtly. 'And I did see it coming.'

'A wayward *career* woman,' said Tristan. 'Now I'm really intrigued. What did *you* offer?'

'Everything,' he muttered.

'Ouch,' said Luke. 'You finished with those darts yet?'

Pete threw his last dart and headed across to the board to retrieve all three of them and mark down his score on the nearby chalkboard. 'You ready to try and hit the dartboard yet, junior, or shall I just save time and mark you down as a no score?' he countered with an edge to his voice that warned Luke that if he wanted a rumble tonight he was going the right way about getting it. But Luke had fallen strangely silent. The room itself felt as if it had drawn a giant breath.

He looked round for the reason for all that silence, and all but swallowed his tongue.

She wore a sky-blue dress that could have been demure but for the perfection of the body beneath it. She was all heavenly curves and sensual grace and as her gaze swept the room several bellies were ruthlessly sucked in, but to no avail.

Her gaze rested on him, her brown eyes thoughtful, and then she smiled; a reckless, challenging smile that promised the kind of trouble a man might just well beg for one more taste of. Someone beside him whimpered. He thought it might have been Luke.

She sauntered towards them, there was no other word for it, and Pete straightened. They all straightened.

'You think that's her?' muttered Tristan.

'He just stabbed himself with the darts,' said Jake. 'It's her.'

The bar was decidedly down-market—a little on the rough side, a little too dark. Serena didn't know what had possessed her to think that walking into a bar like this, *dressed* like this, was a good idea but she tossed her head back and kept right on walking, her eyes firmly fixed on her mark. She'd trawled through the Bennetts in the phone book and finally got lucky in the form of Jake, the brother who usually lived in Singapore but could currently be found manning the family home in Sydney.

He'd given her Pete's phone number, and, just in case she gathered enough courage for it, she'd asked where she might look if she wanted to find Pete in person.

Jake had told her where. And when. But he'd neglected to mention just how many other people might be around. Or how they would stare.

She'd dressed carefully for the occasion. A blue silk sundress, as blue as a summer sky. A first-date dress that flared gently over her hips and ended just above the knee. The strappy bodice favoured skin over fabric, the three little buttons in the middle were a masterful touch and guaranteed to make a man's fingers itch. Her hair fell in waves to her waist and her mouth glowed a shade darker than natural courtesy of some very expensive lipstick. She'd been aiming for elegant sophistication but, judging by the reaction of the crowd, she'd also nailed sexy. Never mind. Faint heart would never hold this man.

Fortunately, she didn't have one.

'Hey, flyboy,' she said when she reached him.

'Serena,' he said gruffly.

She glanced around at the men ranging on either side of him, three of them in total, all of them dangerous-looking enough to make grown women preen and the rest of the patrons in the bar eyeball them carefully. 'Aren't you going to introduce me to your friends?'

'No.'

'Then I'm guessing a drink is out of the question?' she said with the raise of an eyebrow.

'Get her a drink,' said the man to Pete's right, one of Pete's brothers if his dark good looks were any indication.

'Get her a chair,' said another one.

'Get her number,' said the third and winced when Pete dumped the darts into his hand points down.

'What are you doing here?' said the only man whose words she wanted to hear.

'You left without saying goodbye,' she said quietly.

'He usually has better manners,' said one of them.

'Maybe he lost his *mind*,' said another. 'I'm Tristan. This is Jake,' he said, gesturing towards the one she'd pegged earlier as a brother. 'The one with the holes in his hand is Luke.'

Great. *All* of them brothers. Nothing quite like meeting the family *en masse*. 'Gentlemen.' Serena sent them a smile. If she didn't miss her guess, they were giving their man time to regroup. That or deliberately trying to rile him. She didn't mind him riled. She much preferred snarling to cool indifference.

'They were just leaving,' said Pete. 'Now.'

'And miss all this?' said Tristan, sharing a glance with his brothers that had more than a whisper of rogue about it. 'You have *got* to be kidding. I *love* reunions.'

'Then *we're* leaving.' Pete grabbed her by the hand and started dragging her towards the door before she could so much as summon a protest. Not that she felt inclined to protest. Chances were she was about to humiliate herself completely. For that she only needed an audience of one.

Once they were clear of the hotel, he headed for the beach across the road, his stride ground eating and his silence oppressive. He stopped to let her slip off her sandals when they reached the sand and then he was off again, heading towards the water's edge. When he reached it he dropped her hand and shoved both of his in his pockets before turning to face her.

'Why are you here?' he said.

'You asked me a question back on the island. One that took me by surprise. I wasn't expecting it. Didn't know how to answer it.'

His lips twisted. 'You left for Athens two days later, Serena. I thought you answered it fairly comprehensively, all things considered.'

'Then let me ask you a question,' she said. 'If I'd asked you to come with me to Athens…to be with me, build a life with me…would you have?'

He looked at her for what seemed like an eternity, the tension in him a living thing. 'Yes,' he said curtly. 'But you never did ask.'

'Because I knew damn well you needed to be *here*, not there!' she countered, stung by the chill in his eyes.

'I *needed* you. Maybe I didn't make that clear enough for you, Serena. I love you. I'd have done whatever it took to be with you. The only reason I let you go was because I thought you didn't want *me*. That you'd rather be free.' He turned away from her and stared out to sea. 'When my mother died my father took down every picture we had of her and packed them away in a box in the attic. I could never understand why he did it, but I understand now. Lord, it hurts to look at you.'

Three observers stood on the deck of the nearby hotel and watched with varying degrees of concern.

'He's blowing it,' said Luke.

'Have a little faith,' said Tristan.

Jake said nothing.

It wasn't meant to play out like this, thought Serena with increasing desperation. He wasn't supposed to tell her he loved her with one breath and refuse to even look at her the next.

'What happened with the job?' he said abruptly.

'It was a good job, don't get me wrong,' she said. 'For a long time I'd dreamed of landing one just like it, but dreams change.' Serena hesitated, not at all sure of her next move in the face of his continued silence. 'These days I dream of you.'

Desperate times called for desperate measures. She waded out into the water so that she stood in front of him, facing him, her hands on her hips and her chin held high. A wave caught the edges of her dress, lifting it higher, plastering it to her thighs, but she didn't care. A wave could drench her completely and she wouldn't care.

'Your father put those pictures away because he couldn't bear to see what he'd lost,' she told him bluntly. 'You look at me, Pete Bennett. You look your fill because I'm not dead and I'm sure as hell not lost to you. I came here because I wanted to be with you. I want to live with you in your little cottage on the hillside. I can work from home. I can work in Sydney if I've a mind to. I can compromise. Because the most important thing in my life isn't my work…it's you.'

The ghost of a smile touched his lips, reached his eyes, and Serena let out the breath she'd been holding with a shudder. Until the smile in his eyes turned into an all too familiar gleam.

'You love me?' he said.

'I love you,' she told him. 'I'm absolutely stark raving bonkers about you, in case you hadn't noticed.'

'Prove it,' he said. 'Discreetly.'

'We don't do discreet, remember? But for you I'll try.' She knew how to play this game. Damn sure she did. She smiled sweetly as her fingers went to the buttons on her dress, loosing them swiftly before lowering crossed arms to the hem of her dress and peeling it skywards.

Back on the deck Jake choked on the beer he'd just set to his lips.

'Sweet Mary Mother of God,' said Tristan.

'Amen,' muttered Luke.

'Don't panic,' said Jake. 'No need to panic! She *is* wearing swimmers. People do that at the beach. Maybe she just wants to go for a swim to cool off…or something. No one's going to arrest them.' Jake watched with fatalistic resignation as his brother caught her by the waist and tumbled her to the sand, dragging her more or less beneath him, pinning her to the ground. 'Yet.'

'Maybe he'll grow a brain and remember where they are,' said Luke.

'Would you?' countered Tristan.

Luke sighed. 'Maybe *she'll* remember.'

Three men watched in silence as the couple on the beach rolled until Pete lay on his back with Serena plastered all over *him*, in a manner reminiscent of a very old movie.

'She did remember,' said Jake dryly, rolling his eyes. 'That's *so* much better. No way anyone's going to arrest them *now*.'

'I want four children,' said Pete as he wrestled with his libido and the knowledge that if they weren't careful they'd end up making love right there and then.

'You'll get them.' She wound her arms around his neck.

'A garage full of Vespas.'

'That can be arranged.'

'A helicopter on a hillside.'

'Beats driving.'

'Award-winning photographs on the walls.'

'I'll do my best.' His lips scraped over the curve of her jaw, warm and easy. She wanted more. Much *much* more.

'And you.'

A wave rushed up the sand, splashing between them, around them. 'Trust me Pete Bennett,' she murmured, just before his lips found hers, still lazy and teasing but with an edge of hunger in them that made her tremble. 'You'll get that too.'

THE MARRIAGE BARGAIN

Bid for, bargained for, bound forever!

A merciless Spaniard, a British billionaire,
an arrogant businessman and a ruthless tycoon:
these men have one thing in common—they're all
in the bidding for a bride!

There's only one answer to their proposals they'll
accept—and they will do whatever it takes to
claim a willing wife....

**Look for all the exciting stories,
available in June:**

The Millionaire's Chosen Bride #57
by SUSANNE JAMES

His Bid for a Bride #58
by CAROLE MORTIMER

The Spaniard's Marriage Bargain #59
by ABBY GREEN

Ruthless Husband, Convenient Wife #60
by MADELEINE KER

NIGHTS *of* PASSION

One night is never enough!

*These guys know what they want
and how they're going to get it!*

PLEASURED BY
THE SECRET MILLIONAIRE
by Natalie Anderson

Rhys Maitland has gone incognito—he's sick of
women wanting him only for his looks and money!
He wants more than one night with passionate
Sienna, but she has her own secrets….

Book #2834

Available June 2009

**Catch all these hot stories where sparky romance
and sizzling passion are guaranteed!**

REQUEST YOUR FREE BOOKS!

HARLEQUIN *Presents*®

2 FREE NOVELS PLUS 2 FREE GIFTS!

PASSION GUARANTEED SEDUCTION

YES! Please send me 2 FREE Harlequin Presents® novels and my 2 FREE gifts (gifts are worth about $10). After receiving them, if I don't wish to receive any more books, I can return the shipping statement marked "cancel". If I don't cancel, I will receive 6 brand-new novels every month and be billed just $4.05 per book in the U.S. or $4.74 per book in Canada, plus 25¢ shipping and handling per book and applicable taxes, if any*. That's a savings of close to 15% off the cover price! I understand that accepting the 2 free books and gifts places me under no obligation to buy anything. I can always return a shipment and cancel at any time. Even if I never buy another book, the two free books and gifts are mine to keep forever.

106 HDN ERRW 306 HDN ERRL

Name _____ (PLEASE PRINT) _____

Address _____ Apt. # _____

City _____ State/Prov. _____ Zip/Postal Code _____

Signature (if under 18, a parent or guardian must sign)

Mail to the **Harlequin Reader Service:**
IN U.S.A.: P.O. Box 1867, Buffalo, NY 14240-1867
IN CANADA: P.O. Box 609, Fort Erie, Ontario L2A 5X3

Not valid to current subscribers of Harlequin Presents books.

Want to try two free books from another line?
Call 1-800-873-8635 or visit www.morefreebooks.com.

* Terms and prices subject to change without notice. N.Y. residents add applicable sales tax. Canadian residents will be charged applicable provincial taxes and GST. Offer not valid in Quebec. This offer is limited to one order per household. All orders subject to approval. Credit or debit balances in a customer's account(s) may be offset by any other outstanding balance owed by or to the customer. Please allow 4 to 6 weeks for delivery. Offer available while quantities last.

Your Privacy: Harlequin Books is committed to protecting your privacy. Our Privacy Policy is available online at www.eHarlequin.com or upon request from the Reader Service. From time to time we make our lists of customers available to reputable third parties who may have a product or service of interest to you. If you would prefer we not share your name and address, please check here. ☐

HP08R